DEADLY CORRUPTION

Recent Titles by Jeffrey Ashford from Severn House

THE COST OF INNOCENCE
DEADLY CORRUPTION
EVIDENTIALLY GUILTY
FAIR EXCHANGE IS ROBBERY
AN HONEST BETRAYAL
LOOKING-GLASS JUSTICE
MURDER WILL OUT
A TRUTHFUL INJUSTICE
A WEB OF CIRCUMSTANCES

Writing as Roderic Jeffries

DEFINITELY DECEASED
AN INTRIGUING MURDER
SEEING IS DECEIVING
A SUNNY DISAPPEARANCE

DEADLY CORRUPTION

Jeffrey Ashford

This first world edition published in Great Britain 2005 by
SEVERN HOUSE PUBLISHERS LTD of
9–15 High Street, Sutton, Surrey SM1 1DF.
This first world edition published in the USA 2005 by
SEVERN HOUSE PUBLISHERS INC of
595 Madison Avenue, New York, N.Y. 10022.

British Library Cataloguing in Publication Data

Ashford, Jeffrey, 1926-
Deadly corruption
1. Murder - Investigation - Fiction
2. Sailors - Fiction
3. Jewelry theft - Fiction
4. Detective and mystery stories
I. Title
823.9'14 [F]

ISBN 0-7278-6256-1

Except where actual historical events and characters are being described for the storyline of this novel, all situations in this publication are fictitious and any resemblance to living persons is purely coincidental.

Typeset by Palimpsest Book Production Ltd.,
Polmont, Stirlingshire, Scotland.
Printed and bound in Great Britain by
MPG Books Ltd., Bodmin, Cornwall.

One

For once the radar was working and Bazaruto Island was on the screen, its southern tip at 252 degrees and 12 miles. Dunn went through the wheelhouse to the chartroom and used parallel rulers and protractor to plot their position on the chart – the surface of which was badly disturbed from repeated rubbings-out. The *Hakota* had seen too much time and wear.

He looked up at the electric clock on the bulkhead above the chart table. Half an hour to the end of the watch, when he would be relieved. Or wouldn't. It was seldom Moran arrived on the bridge on time. The third officer had developed slackness into a fine art.

He returned to the wheelhouse. Varley, the AB at the helm, turned the wheel a couple of spokes. Because they were slightly off course or he wanted to make it obvious he was alert? If the latter, a wasted effort. Dunn had mentally labelled him an inefficient slacker after a couple of days.

Dunn went out on to the starboard wing. The sea was calm, the swell, slight, the wind, only that produced by the ship's passage; the moon was full and it sent a shaft of light across the water. A scene for young lovers who had yet to learn the harsh truth about love.

He rested his arms on the dodger and stared ahead. He'd recently read that love lay at the crossroads between heaven and hell. A fanciful description, but he went along with it . . .

Minutes, and several memories later, he thought a light

was visible, yet could not be certain. He used the old trick of looking to the side of the possible sighting and this confirmed there was a light. He went into the wheelhouse, picked up the binoculars from the for'd working surface, returned outside. The binoculars were old and faulty, but if one closed the left eye, they offered some visual assistance. He made out the two white masthead lights and one green sidelight of an oncoming vessel. If there was no change of course, they would pass each other in safety. He put the binoculars down. He'd heard the old jingle 'Green to green, red to red, perfect safety, go ahead' on his first day at the training college. They'd also been told by the one-eyed instructor that they would have to learn by heart every one of the Rules of the Road. None of them had realized what a mammoth task that would prove to be. One of the cadets had later said it was not worth the mental effort and had left the college, claiming he was going to open a brothel which would require learning nothing and must prove to be more profitable than sailing the seven seas. Dunn wondered how rich and respected he had become.

There were the sounds of someone climbing the ladder from the boat-deck.

'Evening, sir,' Lynch said, as he stepped up on to the wing.

'Evening.' Lynch was hard working, efficient, and respectful without a hint of brown-nosing. It was unusual to find so solid a hand aboard the *Hakota*.

There was a murmur of conversation from the wheelhouse as the helmsmen changed, then Varley came out on to the wing, crossed to the ladder, and took a step down.

'You might have a report to make?' Dunn asked sarcastically.

'Steady on one eight two,' Varley replied.

'Thank you.'

No doubt, Dunn thought, Varley regarded him as a brass-polisher; acting as if on a luxury cruise liner, not a floating wreck. But discipline and routine were two of the keys to the efficient running of a ship.

A phone rang in the wheelhouse. He went in and in the dim light from the gyro and standard compass binnacles, picked up the first of the three phones on the bulkhead. 'Bridge.'

'It's me on lookout now.'

'Who is me?'

'What's that?'

'Your name?'

'Penn.'

'Thank you.' He replaced the phone back on its stand. Penn was a hulk of a man, light on intelligence, who spoke with a Liverpudlian accent which at times made him almost incomprehensible.

Back on the wing, the lights of the oncoming vessel were now clearly visible. The lookout had not yet reported them, but at night he kept watch from the bows and therefore enjoyed a less distant visibility. The crow's-nest was seldom used.

Dunn paced the wing, fully alert to the present even while his thoughts wandered. If he had remained with the Beltrane Line – correction, if he had been allowed to remain – he would now be in command or only a couple of retirements away from that. The company had a fleet of large container ships, none of which was more than seven years old. The crew were provided with accommodation which only a few years previously would have been deemed unobtainable luxury – this, not because of the company's benevolence, but the difficulty in finding first-class seamen. If he had gained command, he would have been entitled to have Estelle aboard for a trip. Would she then have acted differently?

Moran came out of the wheelhouse on to the wing. Because moonlight softened, his facial appearance lacked the suggestion of slyness it sometimes projected. 'Sorry I'm a touch late, chief.'

'I'm grateful you've finally managed to get here.'

'The stand-by didn't give me a decent call.'

'Suggest he uses cold water next time.'

'They're such a useless bunch of shoreskivers.' Moran leaned against the engine-room telegraph. 'Did I tell you what happened just before we sailed from Cavado?'

'Probably.'

'I couldn't believe my eyes.'

'Advisable.'

'You'll never guess what I saw.'

'Then I won't make the attempt. Have you read the old man's night orders?'

'Yeah.'

'So you'll remember the engine-room ventilators in future?'

'There wasn't enough wind to make any difference whichever way the ventilators were trimmed.'

'It was the order that was important, not the wind.'

'You sometimes say odd things, chief.'

'Hopefully, that prevents me becoming too trite . . . The only vessel in sight is four points out to starboard; our course is one eight two, gyro error one east. I don't think the stand-by has brought up tea yet, so you'd better remind him of the benefits to others of good watch-keeping.'

Dunn was unsurprised that his informal remonstrance went unregistered. Subtlety was not the third's forte. He left the wing, went into the chartroom, blinking rapidly to counter the effects of lighting. At the chart table, he made his entry for the 1600 to 2000 hours watch in the log book.

Moran stepped into the chartroom. 'As I was going to tell you—'

'Is the oncoming ship maintaining her course?'

'I expect so . . . Before we sailed, I was ashore and met the old man. He was in the Gut.'

'What?' Dunn's voice expressed his surprise. The Gut was the name visiting seamen gave the Jaoa Tete area of

Porto Cavado. It was said that there, all a man needed to fulfil his most exotic dreams was ten dollars.

'Raises questions, doesn't it?'

'One of which is, what were you doing there?'

'Just passing through.'

'So why shouldn't he have been doing the same?'

'Because when he recognized me, he looked . . . Furious and embarrassed. Like a man caught giving the au pair a tickle.'

'It might be an idea to forgo any further possibilities and check whether the oncoming vessel is about to ram us.'

Moran was annoyed his potentially salacious news was treated so cavalierly. As Dunn crossed to the doorway, he said: 'I think it's weird even if you don't.'

Dunn left the chartroom, went aft along the short alley to the companionway, down past the captain's flat to the officers' and engineers' accommodation. His cabin was on the starboard side, for'd of the cross-alley. He entered, switched on the overhead light, sat on the chair between the washbasin and the short, uncomfortable settee. Through the opened port came the swishing sounds of their passage through the water. A slightly firmer swell was causing them to roll more noticeably and the hull gently creaked – a sound welcomed by older hands because it meant the ship had been riveted, not welded.

He poured himself a pink gin, drank. He wondered if Estelle had found any difficulty in writing the letter he'd collected from the chief steward's cabin the day they'd arrived. He'd expected to read about the local gossip, the course of her ongoing argument with the local farmer who would not fence in his animals securely, the latest absurdity of Juliet . . . The letter could not have been more atypical. Life had been hard enough when he had worked for the Beltrane Line and everyone they knew earned much more than he did, but when the company had sacked him, the only job he could find had paid even less, so that they had been left virtually in penury. He'd never begun to consider her or he would have realized how desperately lonely she was and how he was never at home when she needed help. She had finally decided that she could no longer be expected to sacrifice her own life. She was leaving the cottage to be with someone who thought of other people. Cedric.

Cedric was wealthy and lived in Kingsford Manor, a seventeenth-century hall house which Estelle had always coveted and about as different as it could be from their twentieth-century, clapboard cottage. Had he been naive not to have imagined the possibility of a relationship between her and Cedric?

He wondered whether to have a second drink, decided not. His wife's extravagance might have left him in serious debt, she might have decided to grant her favours elsewhere, but in seven and a half hours he had to be back on watch, wide awake and sharp eyed. He brushed his teeth, undressed, put on pyjama trousers, pulled back the top sheet because it was too clammily hot for any covering – the primitive air-conditioning didn't work – climbed on to his bunk, picked up a paperback. Minutes later, realizing he was not following what he was reading, he put the book down and switched off the light. If only, he thought, he had in the past enjoyed pleasures generously offered in various ports, he would at least not now suffer the ironic humiliation of being an innocent victim.

Two

They loaded cotton, sugar, sisal, and cashew nuts in Hinde. Being a small port unable to take ships with a draught of more than 15 feet, the *Hakota* anchored offshore and cargo was brought out in lighters. During the course of loading, a runner on the for'd starboard derrick at No. 2 parted and slashed back with such force that it dented the Samson-post; had it swept downwards instead of sideways, at least one man would have been cut in half. Later, a winch broke down and it took the chief electrician over two hours to get it working again.

The company's agent – an expatriate Englishman with good reason for not returning home – sat in the captain's day room and stared down at his empty glass, wondering how long it would take to be offered a refill? 'The mooring and chartering charges will be above estimate and then there's the added stevedoring bills . . .'

The captain stared at the far bulkhead. Head office would blame him for the financial consequences of their problems even though he had repeatedly advised them that the ship was working beyond her capabilities and all her gear needed overhauling.

The agent became resigned to the fact he would not be offered another whisky – a drink which cost a fortune in Hinde. He put his glass down on the small table fastened to the deck, stood. 'I'm afraid I'll have to make it clear in my report that the delays were no fault of ours.'

Like every other bloody shoreman, the captain thought, the fault always lay with someone else.

'I'll be away then. Have a good trip.'

It was an effort to thank him for his good wishes.

The agent left. The captain picked up his cap, jammed it on his head, made his way up to the wheelhouse and through to the starboard wing, where the third was leaning against the dodger. 'Are you too tired to stand?' he demanded.

Moran hurriedly stood upright.

'Are we ready to sail?'

'There's no sign of the pilot yet, sir.'

'Why not?'

'I couldn't say.'

The captain stumped his way to the end of the wing and looked down at the muddy-coloured water that flowed steadily past the hull despite their distance offshore, evidence of the force with which the river ran into the bay. He stamped his way back into the wheelhouse and used the phone to speak to Dunn, standing in the bows. 'Where's the pilot?'

Dunn mistook his voice for the third's because of the distortion. 'How the hell would I know?'

'Does any of my officers know a bloody thing?' he shouted, eliminating the need for the telephone. He returned to the wing, cursing the pilotage service, his officers, the crew. As someone who had once served under him had remarked, it was contrary to nature to find such venom in someone of so insignificant an appearance.

'There's a boat coming out, sir,' the third reported. 'I can't be certain yet if it is the pilot because it's still a way off . . .'

'Who's standing by the ladder?'

'An OS, I expect.'

'You expect? You don't know?'

'The bosun usually details a hand, sir.'

'And you always lack the initiative to check that he has?'

The third remained silent.

'Do you think you're serving on a Thames barge?'

The captain watched the boat come alongside the rope ladder and the pilot begin to climb, then resumed pacing.

The pilot climbed up from the boat-deck to the bridge. 'Afternoon, Captain.' He spoke in a deep, tuneful voice, his English fluent, if heavily accented.

The captain muttered an ungracious reply, his ill-temper increased because the Mozambican was over six feet tall and looked down on him.

'Are you ready to sail, Captain?'

'I've been ready for the past hour and a half.'

The pilot laughed. 'You people are always in a hurry.'

The captain's expression tightened.

'Are the engines on stand-by?'

'Of course.'

'You can raise anchor.'

'Third!'

The third hurried into the wheelhouse and over the phone told the chief officer to start hoisting. In the bows, Dunn moved his hand in a circular movement and the carpenter started the windlass. The anchor chain came up slowly, making a dull, thudding sound each time a link fell into place.

A phone rang in the wheelhouse. The third reported to the pilot. 'Anchor free.'

'Dead slow ahead both,' the pilot ordered.

The third moved the handles on either side of the engine-room telegraphs from stand-by to dead slow ahead; the inner indicators swung round, to the accompaniment of jingling bells, confirming the order had been received.

'Steer one sixty.'

The AB at the helm turned the wheel. 'Steady on one sixty, sir.'

For several minutes, the pilot judged the widening angle

between the remains of the Portuguese fort to port and the end of the sandy spit to starboard. 'Midships.'

A phone rang. The third hurried into the wheelhouse.

'Tell the captain we've lost the anchor,' Dunn said.

'Christ! What happened?'

'The shackle-pin fractured when we were hoisting.'

The third replaced the phone on its hooked stand. As he returned outboard, he decided to leave the mate to report the lost anchor and suffer the consequences of exacerbating the captain's foul temper.

'Stop both,' ordered the pilot.

He crossed to the telegraphs and brought both handles up to the vertical.

The pilot walked to the end of the wing and looked down. 'My boat's alongside.' He returned to where the captain stood. 'Have a good trip.' He leaned forward slightly to shake hands, a thoughtfulness the captain accepted as a gesture of amused contempt.

The third accompanied the pilot down to the main deck and for'd to the rope ladder which was made fast six feet for'd of the accommodation bulkhead. The pilot climbed over the rails, secured a solid footing, and began to descend, then stopped. 'Not a happy ship, I think?' He resumed his descent, moving with an athletic ease which masked the difficulties of what he was doing. He stepped down into the boat and the helmsman advanced the throttle of the outboard as they sheered away to starboard.

The unhappiest ship he'd ever sailed in, the third thought, before giving the order to hoist and secure the ladder. He made his way into the accommodation and had reached the officers' deck when a call from below checked him. He waited for Dunn to join him.

'How did the old man take the news?' Dunn asked.

'As a matter of fact . . . There was so much going on, there wasn't the chance to tell him.'

'Much to your regret?'

The third's expression became resentful.

'I imagine he'll become even less pleased to learn the anchor isn't buoyed.'

'Why's that?'

'The line parted when the shackle collapsed, so the buoy drifted off.'

'He'll throw a fit.'

'Perhaps I can ease his pain by pointing out that nothing is lost if one knows where it is. As the cabin boy said to the captain after accidentally dropping his silver teapot over the side in the middle of the Atlantic.'

The third wondered how the mate could joke about a catastrophe.

'But at least there shouldn't be any trouble in finding the anchor even if it isn't buoyed. How long after we were under way did I report the loss?'

'Three, four minutes.'

'Speed?'

'Dead slow.'

'That's two knots. Course?'

'I can't remember.'

'It'll be down in the Movements Book, provided, that is, you weren't too busy to note down all helm, speed, and engine orders?'

'Of course I did.'

'Then with a sandy bottom, there shouldn't be any problem.'

When Dunn entered the captain's day cabin, he was surprised to see the tiger there. Tucker was a runt of a man – some three to four inches shorter than the captain – and dark, sparse ginger hair, wide set eyes, one of which had a drooping eyelid, a nose which had been broken and badly reset, and a thin-lipped mouth, melded into a face which made one doubt that even his mother had ever thought him handsome. Because of his familiar attitude towards the captain, often expressing himself in a way that had any other member of the crew spoken in similar terms, he would have been damned to hell for his insolence, their relationship was the subject of bawdy speculation. Dunn was certain that was nonsense. Tucker's position was that of a traditional court jester.

'Where's your report?' the captain demanded as he sat in front of his desk.

Dunn handed over the sheet of paper on which, three-fingered, he had typed out the details of the loss of the anchor.

The captain gave his opinion without reading the report. 'Sheer bloody inefficiency.'

'Hardly that . . .'

'Even a cadet has enough sense to make certain an anchor's securely buoyed.'

'Which it was, but the line parted under the stress when the pin fractured.'

'You should have checked anchor and cable before the anchor was dropped.'

Dunn's resentment increased, not because of the captain's attitude – that was to be expected – but because he was being criticized in front of Tucker.

'Did you examine the line before it was attached to the anchor?'

'Yes, sir.'

'Then you did so incompetently.'

'I decided it needed replacing, but Lamps had no fresh line in store.'

'If a requisition had been put in previously for new line, this would not have happened.'

'If ifs and ands were pots and—' Tucker began, his voice reedy.

'You can clear out,' the captain snapped.

'I ain't going anywheres until you say if you wants the meal up here or below.'

'I've already told you.'

'You said you didn't know, what wasn't no help.'

'I'll eat up here.'

'Not feeling very social, aren't we?'

'Clear off.'

Tucker left and closed the door behind himself.

'What is head office going to say when I tell them we've lost an anchor?' the captain said angrily.

There was some perverse satisfaction, Dunn thought, to be gained from the knowledge that ashore, a captain was no longer God, unchallengeable. 'It should be recovered easily since we can accurately pinpoint its position using time and speed from the anchor bearings.'

'That will hardly blind them to your inefficiency.'

'If head office maintained their ships in good condition, we wouldn't have to suffer rotting lines, snapping runners, winches which constantly break down, and an almost total lack of stores.'

'A bad workman blames his tools.'

'So does a good workman when they're no damned good.'

Dunn left and went down to his cabin. He sat in the battered – but comfortable – chair and stared through the port at the dull curtain of rain beyond the ship. It was difficult to accept it was only two years since he had served on the *Calliope* – a modern vessel of twenty thousand tons with a captain who chose to treat his officers with pleasant and fair authority, officers who were proud of their jobs and their ship, and a crew who were efficient.

Three

On the morning of the third day out, they ran into fog. The captain was a seaman and the delays they had suffered when unloading and loading meant they were not keeping to their schedule, but he refused to take any risks in order to make up time. A daytime lookout was posted at the bows, the automatic foghorn control was engaged, speed was severely reduced, the radar screen was constantly checked, and the captain remained on the bridge throughout the day and night.

By four in the morning, their speed remained at four knots. A lazy swell from the east kept the *Hakota* rolling and anything loose was in danger of being thrown to the deck. Dunn climbed the companionway up to the chartroom, where he checked the captain's Night Orders Book – there was no entry – read the barometer, carried on through to the wheelhouse. The captain was just visible. 'Good morning, sir.'

There was a grunted reply.

He checked the radar, picked up a cup of tea and a sandwich from the tray brought by the stand-by, went out on to the starboard wing. The second, who had been pacing, came to a stop.

'There's no sign of a break, then?' Dunn said, as he stared out at the blanket of fog, coloured green by the sidelight.

'Not the sniff of one. And if it goes on too long like this, we're going to arrive home so late I'll miss Rosie's birthday, which will be disastrous. Wives get so sentimental about birthdays. Come to that, about everything.'

Except their husbands, he thought as he bit into the sandwich. The bread was stale and the filling a paste of indeterminate origin.

'I promised to take her to Calais for the day as a birthday present, provided she finds someone to look after the kids.'

The foghorn sounded and Dunn waited for it to cease before he asked: 'She likes France?'

'We both do. Occasionally we take Eurostar and have a wander and a meal: a couple of trips back, we found a small family restaurant which serves grub one dreams about. Then the last leave, we motored down to Malmaux. Rosie fell in love with the place and said we had to buy a holiday home there. Didn't suggest what we'd use for money when it's a job to keep our heads above water even with both of us earning.'

'Ever thought of moving to France?'

'Sure. It would be great, just so long as there weren't any French around.'

'Rather a difficult condition to meet!'

'They can be so rude when you don't speak their lingo . . . Where do you go when you're back home?'

'My pleasure is relaxing in the sitting room and not giving a damn if the wind's rising, the deck's not been holystoned, and the lookout's blind drunk.'

'Doesn't the wife shout she wants to go out and have fun?'

'Not any more,' he answered, with sharp, brief bitterness.

'Then you're lucky. I reckon one of Rosie's ancestors was an explorer – always wants to be on the move. Not that she'd make much of an explorer. Sees a slow-worm and it's an anaconda.'

'Do you think this is a tea party?' demanded the captain

from the doorway of the wheelhouse. He stepped out on to the wing. 'You're supposed to be keeping a lookout, not gossiping like old women.'

They remained silent until the second said to Dunn: 'Course two one five, forty revs. The gyro error couldn't be checked. One ship visible on radar on the port beam, proceeding northwards at a distance of eleven miles.'

'OK.'

The second went inside.

The captain walked to the end of the wing, urinated into the scupper, turned. 'I expect my chief officer to set an example, not encourage slackness by example. This isn't a bloody tug boat.'

Dunn wondered why tug boats and barges featured so frequently in the other's diatribes.

'Have you bothered to check the radar?'

The foghorn sounded and Dunn had to wait until it was over before saying: 'When I came on watch, sir.'

'There's a ship out to port.'

'So I saw and as the second has just reported.'

'In fog conditions, the radar is to be checked very regularly. You've been gossiping for so long you can have no idea of what she's doing.'

Talking for five minutes, Dunn judged. Unless the other ship had turned about and was jet-propelled, there was no danger of collision. But the old saying held wisdom. It was more important to appear to be doing something than actually doing it. He went into the wheelhouse, put his empty mug on the tray, checked the radar screen. It was free of blips. He returned outside. 'No vessel on radar, sir.'

'Maintain a better watch,' the captain said before he went into the wheelhouse.

Although the night was warm, the fog had brought a raw dampness to the air and Dunn began to pace the wing. Was the captain bloody-minded through nature or nurture? And what had reduced him to command of the *Hakota*? Had he also suffered from circumstances?

When some time later, Dunn went through to the chart room, the captain was slumped on the settee, asleep, exhausted by endless hours on the bridge. It would have been satisfying to wake him and suggest he kept a better watch. Dunn returned to the starboard wing. The green-tainted fog held a suggestion it was beginning to thin. He leaned on the dodger and let his mind wander as his senses remained alert. His mother had made no secret of the fact that in her opinion, Estelle would not make a good wife. She dressed expensively, was always wanting to go out to a meal, the theatre, a dance, and unable to appreciate it was more difficult to earn a pound than to spend one. He had, of course, assumed her criticisms to be those of a mother for whom not even Venus would be good enough for her son. It had taken him a long time to realize she had been correct . . . He chanced to look aft and saw a man coming for'd along the boat-deck. Fog, if thinning, still distorted and although he thought the man was Tucker, going to see what the captain wanted, he could not be certain.

At six, the stand-by brought tea – weak – and sandwiches – stale – up to the bridge. Dunn carried a mug of tea and a sandwich out on to the wing; a moment later, the captain followed him.

'Nothing in sight, sir,' Dunn said, 'and the fog seems to be thinning.'

'I've got to go below. Keep a sharp lookout.'

'Sir.'

The captain returned into the wheelhouse.

Dunn let his thoughts wander once more. Did Estelle expect Cedric to remain faithful when he had married three times between affairs? Probably. She usually managed to believe what she wanted to believe.

Growing daylight confirmed the fog was lifting. Hopefully, the foghorn could soon be switched off and its mournful blasts – a chorus of drowned sailors – could be stilled and revs increased. Not that he had any reason to welcome a quick return to cruising speed. The sooner they arrived in England, the sooner he would face an empty home. And every time he drove into Stitchford, he would have to pass the wrought-iron gates of Kingsford Manor.

The third, only five minutes late, came out on to the wing. 'Thank God the fog's all but lifted so the old man won't be on the bridge all morning. Last night, it was like we were in the Channel with a dozen ships up our stern – had I checked this, had I checked that, had the lookout reported, what was the barometer doing, what were the revs.'

'Better safe than sinking.'

'Sure, but why can't he accept we are safe because I'm doing my job properly?'

'It would be tactless of me to suggest an answer . . . There were no star sights, so if it becomes possible, make certain you get a good sun one.'

'Why the hell don't we have a GPS system?'

'Costs money. In any case, the old man would still insist we took sights. He doesn't believe in progress.'

The third leaned against the engine-room telegraphs. 'You'd think from the way he goes on, this was the nineteenth century.'

'The sharper a ship's run, the safer she is.'

'Does he have to be so bloody tempered running her?'

'That also is conforming to tradition . . . I'm away below. Course two one five, revs forty.'

The foghorn sounded.

'Why are we still steaming like visibility's nil?'

'I tried to ask him over the voice pipe for permission to turn it off and increase revs, but he didn't answer.'

'Fast asleep.'

'Wouldn't you be in his shoes?'

'I wouldn't have been on the bridge all night. I'd trust my officers.'

'He finds that rather more difficult than you obviously would.'

'Miserable old sod! It's vinegar in his veins, not blood.'

'So cut one of your veins and what would come out?'

'How d'you mean?'

Dunn went through to the wheelhouse and double-checked his log entry, then below to his cabin. He washed and shaved, made his way down to the saloon for breakfast, after which he would return to the bridge to relieve the third for his meal. The second, the wireless officer, and the chief engineer (the only engineer who ate with the deck officers; oil and water did not mix in a ship of *Hakota*'s agc) were present, but conversation was sparse – they had little in common with each other.

Dunn returned to the bridge to relieve the third. The sky was now almost cloudless, the sun warm, the horizon sharply defined, and the force 2/3 wind barely ruffled the surface of the sea. Flying fish, disturbed by the creaming bow-wave, skimmed the water, frequently glinting in the sunlight; on their starboard bow, dolphins, surfacing and diving with carefree pleasure, kept pace with them. The kind of day when it wasn't all that naive to talk about the romance of the sea.

The foghorn sounded yet again. He unplugged the captain's voice pipe and blew. There was no response. Since there was nothing in sight, he went into the wheelhouse and spoke to the man at the helm. 'I'll take over whilst you go below and tell the captain I've been trying to speak to him over the voice pipe.'

When Varley left the wheelhouse, the gyro repeater ticked as their heading moved to two one six. Dunn put on one spoke of port wheel, held it for thirty seconds, returned the wheel amidships. Hydraulic rams aft had taken the need for strength out of steering, but there was still satisfaction in leaving a straight wake.

He heard the sounds of someone racing up the

companionway. Varley rushed into the wheelhouse with such speed he had to steady himself on the standard compass binnacle. 'He's laid out on deck. I reckon he's a goner.'

Four

Rodgers, the chief steward, was a mournful man. He had a friendly nature and was honest, but – like all chief stewards – knew the crew disliked him because they were convinced they suffered since he was always on the fiddle. He looked at the captain, who lay face downwards on the deck, arms sprawled out. The back of the head was a mess of blood, sodden hair and skull. 'Gawd, what happened?'

'He must have suffered a heart attack and fallen back on to the table,' Dunn replied.

The chief steward looked at the small, square table, its corners strengthened with metal, which was secured to the deck. The nearest corner to the body was heavily stained with blood over a wide area. 'I . . . I need a drink or my guts will blow.'

'First—'

'In the cabin,' he muttered as he hurried across to the doorway and out.

Dunn locked the door, made his way down to the chief steward's cabin on the main deck. Rodgers put down the glass he had just emptied. 'I needed that, no mistake. The sight of blood always . . . What'll you have?'

'A pink gin, please.' It was strange how the mind could work when stressed. For the first time in years, Dunn recalled his father warning him that the man who began to drink before midday would not have finished before midnight.

'Make yourself room to sit.'

The settee was stacked with files and folders – part of

the chief steward's job was to deal with some of the paperwork concerning cargo loaded and discharged – and he had some difficulty in clearing sufficient space.

The chief steward poured several drops of bitters into a glass, revolved the glass to spread them, added a large measure of gin. 'Do you want water?'

'As much again.'

He handed Dunn the glass, refilled his own with a larger measure of whisky, sat.

'Is it true you've met something like this before?' Dunn asked.

'On the *Taranangi*, only it wasn't the old man, it was one of the greasers. Name of Fred, I seem to recall. Got tighter than a virgin's joy and said he was going to tell the chief engineer just what kind of a shit he was. Fred's feet got mixed up and he fell down on to the main deck, for'd of number four. His face looked like . . . Rather not say.'

'What action did the captain take?'

'Ordered the body to be kept frozen so there'd be something for the family ashore. And all the thanks he got for thinking of them was to be bollocked by the law.'

'Why?'

'Hadn't taken any statements at the time. But since all anyone could say was Fred had been blind drunk, what good would that have been?'

'Did the police carry out an investigation?'

'A couple of smart-arsed detectives came aboard and asked questions. One of 'em kept wanting to know if I'd supplied Fred with the booze. I told him, all I passed out was what the company said as I could.'

'Was there an inquest?'

'Must have been, I suppose.'

'You weren't called?'

'Don't remember being.'

The police would want statements, Dunn thought. 'We're going to have to take what evidence we can. I saw him just after six on the bridge; did anyone see him after that? His tiger may well have done. Did anyone hear him complain of not feeling well? . . . Those questions need answers. Get that organized, will you?'

'But—'

'What about the body? Can you keep it frozen like you said it was on the *Taranangi*?'

'We've only the one freezer, so unless it's put in with the grub, there's no way,' Rodgers answered sullenly, annoyed at the extra work he had been given.

'Then we'll have to bury him at sea.' Dunn drained his glass. 'Assuming there'll be an inquest when we get back, they're going to want to know how the captain was, so it'll be an idea to photograph the cabin. Do you know of anyone with a camera?'

'Alf has all the gear – he's a maniac for photography.'

'Who's Alf?'

'The butcher.'

A balding man of considerable substance. 'Ask him to have a word with me as soon as possible.' He stood, put down his empty glass.

'What a bleeding mess!'

In the circumstances, a very appropriate comment, Dunn thought.

'I've always said, she never has been and never will be a happy ship.'

Dunn left and went out on deck, made his way to the carpenter's shop, for'd of the steering flat. The carpenter – the scar on his right cheek gave him a lopsided face; in Buenos Aires, a señorita's boyfriend had unexpectedly returned – was working at his bench. 'We're going to have to have the burial at sea,' Dunn said.

'Aye.'

'Have you enough canvas?'

The carpenter leaned back, hands in the small of his back to relieve pain. 'There's an old hatch cover that's half rotten, but will do. I've asked ashore for new canvas time and again, but it's never come.'

'Can you knock up something on which the body can be rested while I read the service?'

'I reckon.'

'How long will it take to be ready?'

'A couple of hours.'

Dunn looked at his watch. 'We'll have the service at eight bells.'

He returned for'd past the three after hatches and climbed the ladders to the boat-deck. He stopped abeam of number six boat and stared at the deck houses, funnel, bridge, and the foremast, whose crown was lazily drawing circles in the sky as the ship rolled rhythmically. Yesterday, ultimate responsibility for the ship and crew had been with the captain; today, it was with him. Because the sea was forever treacherous, he might at any moment have to make a decision which would decide life and death for many. It was soul-clenching knowledge, but he accepted it without fear. He was trained to command.

The carpenter had made a crude ramp from four-by-four dunnage. A traditionalist, after stitching up the canvas, he had passed the needle through the captain's nose.

The engines were stopped; the red ensign was hoisted at the mainmast, then lowered to half mast; the bosun, carpenter, lamptrimmer, chief engineer, and three deck hands, stood around Dunn as he read from the small booklet which listed forms of prayers to be used at sea. The wind had risen and the ship was moving sufficiently for the carpenter to need to place a hand on the canvas to steady it.

'. . . We therefore commit his body to the deep, to be turned into corruption, looking for the resurrection of the body when the sea shall give up her dead.'

The carpenter gave the canvas a push; it slid along the ramp and, in a narrow arc, fell into the sea, raising a splash which sent three flying fish skimming across the surface.

As Dunn made his way up to the bridge to enter details of the funeral in the log, he wondered why a body had to be corrupted before its resurrection.

Five

Marr slapped his hand down on the light blue TS14a form on the desk. 'Have you any idea what the guv'nor would say if I handed him this?'

Not a second Shakespeare, Helen decided.

'Didn't they teach you anything at that school except how to do the flowers when the Queen's coming to grub?'

They had not been taught flower-arranging at Académie de Elisabeth Chevènement.

'What's the name of the third assailant?'

'I don't know because—'

'You forgot to ask.'

'He ran off while I was coping with the girl. She was like a wildcat.'

'Which surprised you because you expected her to behave like a lady and just spit?'

She sighed. Marr had resented her presence from the day she had joined the CID. In his opinion, even a tax assessment was more welcome than a female. His resentment had become still greater when he had learned she had spent some years at a Swiss school, imagining it to have taught the daughters of the idle rich, rather than being a state school. She had tried to correct his mistake, but he had chosen to remain ignorantly biased. However, he was not all bad news. He did keep his hands to himself. Having met his wife, she felt certain his restraint came from a sense of self-preservation rather than gentlemanly propriety.

'Naturally,' he continued sarcastically, 'you were struggling too hard with the Amazon queen to note which way he ran?'

'Down Church Lane.'

'It didn't occur to you it would be an idea to mention that fact in your report?'

'I thought I had.'

'If ever you start doing instead of thinking, you'll maybe make a policeman of yourself before you retire.'

It was typical of him to say 'policeman' and not 'policewoman'.

'How do you spell receive?'

She answered.

'Then why add an extra *e* in your report?'

'A typing error.'

'You couldn't be bothered to check what you'd written? You don't remember what the guv'nor said about slackness?'

Since the detective inspector had said the same thing many, many times, it was not something one readily forgot.

'Take your report away, retype it, and when you're quite certain there are no omissions or mistakes, give it back to me.' He pushed the form across the desk.

She picked it up, turned, and walked towards the door.

'Hang on.'

She stopped and turned back.

'First, you can get down to the docks.'

She waited, knowing he wanted her to ask why, thereby confirming a woman was more inquisitive than a monk in a nunnery.

Marr reluctantly said: 'A ship's docked on which the captain died from a fall and was buried at sea. The guv'nor wants someone to go aboard and look out the information needed at the inquest, so you can do that. Provided, of course, you don't find it demeaning to have to mix with common seamen.'

'What's the ship's name?'

He searched amongst the papers on his desk, found the one he wanted. '*Hakota*.'

'It's foreign?'

'English. Hoping to find yourself some exotic oo-la-la, were you?'

'Hoping someone on it would speak recognizable English.'

'Didn't they teach you half a dozen languages at that poncey school?'

'Tell me something, sarge. Why does it get right up your nose that I went to a school in Switzerland?'

He didn't answer. She left.

Yates, the only other DC present in the CID general room, looked up as she entered. 'Do you by any chance have a stout poker?'

'Do I look ambidextrous?' She had quickly learned that to become a member of the team, she had to accept her colleagues' vulgarity and, to gain their respect, return it. Women police officers who complained about sexual harassment were unpopular.

'I need one to smash this bloody machine.'

She was amused to learn his question had, for once, been innocuous. 'What's the problem?'

'Been working for almost an hour and then everything goes black because I pressed the wrong tit.'

'Still in too much of a hurry?'

'You're a genius with these machines. They sit up and beg for you. Be a real sport and do the work for me – won't take fifteen minutes.'

'When it's taken you almost an hour?'

'I'm slow, you're fast.'

'You're a liar and an optimist . . . Sorry, Shamus, but I'm on my way to the docks.'

'What's happening there?'

'The captain of a ship that's just docked died and was

buried at sea. I have to gather up information for the inquest.'

'Remembering a case I had a couple of years back, nothing, but nothing, is more important to the court than the exact spot at which the body was dumped over the side. So don't forget to nail that down. What's the name of the ship?'

'*Hakota*. Sounds foreign, but the sarge says it's British.'

'She, Helen, she.'

'She what?'

'A ship is always feminine. Do you want to know why?'

'No, but I'm sure you're going to tell me.'

'The more screws she has, the faster she moves.'

'Male fantasy.'

'What company is she from?'

'The sarge didn't say.'

'At a guess, the Akitoa Shipping Company. They name their ships after places in the south island of New Zealand; the first chairman was from Invercargill.'

'How come you know that obscure piece of information?'

'Always been interested in ships. As a matter of fact, there was a time when I thought of going to sea.'

She crossed to his desk and sat on the edge. 'Your shameful past at last coming to light. Why didn't you enjoy life in a dirty British coaster with a salt-caked smokestack?'

'I recovered my common sense.'

'Not for long or you wouldn't have joined the police.'

He was silent for a moment, then said: 'Akitoa Shipping is something of an anomaly. They started tramping way back and have remained in it when virtually every other British shipping company has long since moved out or disappeared. Rather like the Erickson square-riggers at the outbreak of the last war, their ships are relics from the past. But at least they look like ships.'

'What does that mean?'

'Clean decks, midships superstructure and funnel, built to ride out a real storm. Modern liners look like blocks of flats and container ships, mobile junk heaps. If any cruise liner gets caught up in a real gale, she'll founder.'

'You've got me thinking twice about booking a state-room on the *Arcadia* for a round-the-world cruise.'

The door opened and Marr, standing in the doorway, stared balefully at Helen. 'Busy, are we?'

'Learning all about the *Hakota*, sarge. Shamus is a fundy on ships and shipping companies.'

'More like a fundy on doing nothing . . . Is it too much to ask you to do as ordered?'

She slid off the desk and stood.

Marr spoke to Yates. 'What's happened to your report on the latest mugging in the High Street?'

'I'm working on it.'

'When you can find the time.' He looked around the room. 'Why's this place in a mess?'

'Busy days.'

'What's that silver doing on Trevor's desk?'

'It's from the Lackstone job.'

'I didn't think it was out of an Xmas cracker. Why isn't it locked away?'

'Trevor was drawing up descriptions for the stolen antiques list when he was suddenly called out.'

'And it didn't occur to him to return it under lock and key as rules demand?'

'Since I'm here to make certain it doesn't walk—'

'And when you're suddenly called out?'

'I'll return it before I rush out.'

'And pigs have wings.' Marr looked around the room again. 'Get this cleared up.' He left and slammed the door so hard, a photograph fluttered down from the notice-board.

'How to bring sunshine into our lives,' she said. 'I suppose I'd better start moving or he'll have me booked for desertion.'

'Do me a favour while you're aboard. Have a whisper with the chief steward and ask what are the chances of a few duty-free fags.'

'Customs are bound to have been aboard.'

'Chief stewards always squirrel away fags and booze to sell ashore when it's safe. How else can they afford to live in the luxury to which they've accustomed themselves?'

She walked between the desks, avoiding a pile of folders on the floor which had toppled into an untidy heap, picked up the photograph which had fallen from the notice-board. One of several men pictured had his head ringed in red ink and there was a request for possible identification. She pinned the photograph back in place, next to a handwritten notice reminding everyone that a social evening was being held on the 30th. She wondered whether to go to it. After Dean had left, she had assured herself she wasn't lonely, she was modern woman, very happy to enjoy the freedom of being on her own. She would have liked to believe herself.

The lift was still not working. As she climbed down the first flight of stairs, she wondered if the coming social evening would be any more enjoyable than the last one. All she had gained from that had been an offer of a quickie in the deserted conference room.

Dunn watched the marine superintendent walk down the gangway and across to the parked car by the side of the cargo shed. Captain Barton had expressed regret at having to ask the chief officer temporarily to forgo his leave, but someone had to complete Captain Sewell's voyage work. He had sounded genuinely apologetic, which was strange for a marine superintendent.

Dunn returned to his cabin, sat, poured himself a drink. If he were honest, he wasn't very worried about having his leave delayed. It prolonged the time before he drove past

Kingsford Manor and returned to an empty house. He drank. Yet again, he wondered if Estelle was as happy as she had expected, was still convinced Cedric would not dump her when he tired of her. When dumped, would she want to return and plead for forgiveness? How would he respond? He was damned if he knew. He drained the glass, poured himself another pink gin.

There was a knock on the half-opened door. An OS – whose name he could never remember – said: 'Someone to see you.'

A woman stepped into the cabin. Dunn stood and, presuming she was from the shore office even though she was neatly dressed, said: 'If you've come for the voyage report—'

'Detective Constable Ryan, local CID.'

'Oh!' Surprise momentarily left him confused.

'I understand you are the captain?'

'Acting captain. Felix Dunn.'

'I have to make some enquiries into the death of Captain Sewell in order to prepare evidence for the inquest; I'd be grateful for any help you can give me.'

'No problem. Sit down and what can I offer you to drink?'

'I'll sit, but I don't think I'll have a drink, thanks all the same.' She settled on the settee, looked around herself. 'Is this a very old boat?'

'Pretty long in the keel, but she doesn't quite go back to the days when criminals were given the choice of going to jail or to sea.'

'I've always doubted that actually happened.'

'Judging by some of the crew one sees these days, I'd say it's still being surreptitiously pursued.'

She smiled.

Her smile brought warmth to her round face. Not beautiful, her features possessed an elfish touch to provide charm and suggest she enjoyed the quirks of life. Estelle also had black curly hair, but there was nothing elfish about her. One added an *s* to provide an accurate description.

'Have I powdered my nose too generously?'

'I'm sorry,' he said hastily. 'You remind me of someone and I was trying to work out who.'

'I'm glad I won't know if the comparison is to my advantage or disadvantage,' she said briskly. 'Perhaps it will be best if I outline the information I need and we find out if you can answer any or all of the questions. Where did the captain die?'

'In his day room.'

'Who found him?'

'AB Varley.'

'Tell me the circumstances.'

'We'd been running in thick fog, but that was clearing. I was on watch and decided we could safely stop sounding the foghorn, twice tried to contact the captain on the voice pipe down to his quarters to ask if he'd agree. I couldn't get an answer, so eventually I sent Varley below to check what was happening. He reported back that the captain was lying on the deck, dead.'

'He said the captain was dead or that he was badly injured and might be dead?'

'Thought he was a goner.'

'What did you do?'

'Called up the chief steward and together we went into his quarters. The captain had fallen on the edge of the table in his day room and that had smashed the back of his skull.'

'You could be certain he was dead?'

'Even without any medical knowledge beyond the usual Red Cross first-aid course, there couldn't be much doubt because of the state of his head and the look of him. I think the photos will make that clear enough.'

'What photos?'

'I had a member of the crew take several of him.'

'Why did you do that?'

'The chief steward sailed on a ship where a slightly similar incident occurred and he advised me we should take statements from anyone who could give relevant information because there would be an inquest. It occurred to me that photos might be equally necessary.'

'You were quite right . . . May I see the photos and the statements, please?'

He handed her a large brown envelope. 'The chief steward typed out the statements so they'd be legible; the signed originals are also there.'

He watched her bring out the statements. She frowned slightly as she read. Because she needed glasses or merely an unrecognized habit? Estelle needed glasses when she read, but refused to wear them. Glasses made people look frowzy.

She put the statements down on the settee, brought the photographs out of the envelope.

'They're rather disturbing,' he said.

'Thanks for the warning, but I will probably have seen worse.'

She studied each photograph, returned them all to the envelope. 'I'll take everything with me, but first I'd like a word with the chief steward and Varley.'

'I'll get someone to call them.' He stood. 'I hope I managed to do all that was wanted? It was rather by guess and by God.'

'If everyone were as wide awake as you've been, Captain Dunn, I reckon there'd be times when we wouldn't have anything to do.'

It was good for the ego to be called 'Captain' even if he was not entitled to the rank.

Forty minutes later, he escorted Helen to the gangway. She thanked him for his help. He watched her descend, gripping the top ropes with landlubberly need. Her brightly coloured skirt tightened first to the right, then to the left, in rhythm with her legs . . . She had a neat bottom.

Six

'Well?' said Yates, as Helen stepped into the CID general room.

'Dunn, the acting captain, took statements and photographs at the time of the captain's death. My job was as good as done for me.'

'Never mind all that. What about the fags?'

She had forgotten his request.

'Did the chief steward come across?'

'He said he couldn't be a party to an illegal act.'

'Then he's even more of a hypocrite than usual,' Yates said bad-temperedly.

She sat at her desk. 'I had to do a fair bit of walking in the docks because I started off at the wrong berth – my feet are killing me.'

'Will it help if I massage your legs?'

'Help you do what?'

Horne, tall, thin, and as earnest as his appearance suggested, hurried into the room. 'The bastard!'

'Which one of that very extensive species are we about to discuss?' Yates asked.

'The sarge has just told me to draw up a list county HQ is shouting for. I said, I'm already snowed under with work, but would he listen? Not bloody likely.' He sat. 'I suppose . . .'

'How right you are,' Yates said hurriedly.

'If he did his share of work instead of shoving everything on to us, life would be a hell of a lot easier.'

'If he retired, it would be easier still and much more pleasant.'

'Is he in his room?' Helen asked.

'He was a moment ago when he showed his indifference to my suffering.'

'I'll have a word with him.' She picked up the envelope in which were statements and photographs, crossed between the desks to the door.

'If your feet are still aching on your return,' Yates called out, 'my offer's still wide open.'

'Unlike my legs.'

She went along the narrow corridor to the next room; the sergeant was not there. She turned, to see the detective inspector as he rounded the corner and strode towards her.

'You've been down to the ship?' Tait asked, as he approached her.

She pressed against the wall to allow him to pass. 'I'm just back from it.'

'You can give me a report.' He went into his room.

She could never make up her mind how she judged him. Of medium height and build, balding, he was by nature cold and either unable or unwilling to display the friendly authority which increased a team's efficiency and willingness to work that little bit harder. It was said that in part his manner was due to the fact he was now too old to expect promotion, yet some of his contempories were in high places.

He settled behind his desk. 'Let's have it.'

She considered his face unfinished, as if the sculptor had become bored and moved on to other work: eyes, cheekbones, nose, and mouth seemed slightly out of proportion to each other. 'I spoke to Mr Dunn, the acting captain. He had statements taken at the time of the captain's death and also photographs of the dead man.'

'Good God! . . . Maybe he'll write the report and save us any work at all.'

'It seems the chief steward had previously been on a boat in which something similar occurred and he suggested what to do. I questioned one or two of the crew to check certain points in their statements, otherwise there wasn't much for me to do.'

'It's all straightforward, then?'

She hesitated.

'Inconsistencies in the statements? It would be astonishing if there weren't any.'

'They're all broadly in line.'

'Then where's the problem?'

'If there is one, it's in the photographs.' She stepped forward and handed them to him.

He studied them. 'Who took these?'

'The butcher. A keen amateur who had all his kit with him.'

He put the photos down on the desk, leaned back in the chair. 'So tell me what's bothering you?'

'The photos appear to make it obvious the captain fell heavily backwards on to the edge of the table. But according to the log book – I've made a note of the entry – at the time, the wind and swell were slight. I asked Mr Dunn what that meant in practical terms and he said the ship was barely pitching or rolling. So why should the captain have fallen so hard?'

'He slipped on something or was tight.'

'The tiger says the floor was as clean as it could be, there's no carpet to slide on, and both he and the chief steward agree the captain never drank when at sea.'

'Who – or what – is the tiger?'

'That's what the captain's steward is called . . . The wound makes it clear the captain fell backwards with very considerable momentum; it then seems he collapsed on to the floor, face down, arms outstretched wide. Yet one would have expected him to try to lessen the impact of the fall, in which case one or both arms would probably have ended under him and certainly not outstretched.'

'With a blow that severe, he might have been incapable of trying to save himself. Again, can one ever be certain how the limbs will end up after a fall?'

'Then there's the blood. The photos show the blood stretching up to a foot and a half in from the edge of the table.'

'After a wound that serious, one bleeds.'

'But to leave so much blood over so large an area, surely the head would have had to be over the table for an appreciable time. But he must have struck the table and collapsed to the floor. Another thing. There's no indication of hair or gunge from the inside of the head amongst the blood.'

'A photo can fail to show detail.'

'When it's that clear and close-to? And both the chief steward and Mr Dunn agree there was no sign of any contaminant in the blood.'

'Faced with a gruesome emergency, the amateur can completely miss the obvious.'

'I still think . . .' She stopped.

'Well?'

'There's something wrong, sir.'

He picked up each photo again and examined it. 'So what do you propose?' he asked as he put down the last one.

'An investigation to confirm or deny accidental death.'

'On such doubtful premisses? When we're overburdened with work due to the government's appetite for paperwork and my budget is looking more and more threadbare?'

She said nothing.

He looked up at her, then back at the top photograph. 'Make it short and sharp. And try to remember how to spell "receive" when you make your written report.'

She left, silently describing Marr in terms of which the Académie de Elisabeth Chevènement would not have approved. Mentioning her typing error to the DI had been the act of a small, mean mind.

Some fifteen minutes later, when she was about to leave the CID general room to go down to the canteen for a quick meal, Marr looked in, saw her, and said harshly: 'My room. Now.' He disappeared.

Wiseman – slanderously said by his colleagues to have a name which breached the trade descriptions acts – said: 'What have you done this time?'

'Probably used too much lipstick.'

Marr was not in his room. She stared at the framed photograph of his wife on the desk, on which everything was placed with geometric precision, and wondered if Hilda sometimes wondered why she'd married.

Marr entered, hurried past her, sat behind his desk. 'What the hell do you think you've been up to?'

'Nothing exciting, unfortunately.'

'You've made me look a right charlie.'

He seldom needed help for that.

'Not a word before you go in and report to the DI, so he thinks you must have spoken to me first. Which leaves me not knowing what he's talking about.'

'I tried to have a word with you as soon as I got back, sarge, but you weren't in this room and—'

'And you seized the chance to rush off and tell him what a genius you are.'

'I was walking back from here to our room when he stopped me and said I was to report to him then and there.'

'And so you told him a load of imaginative balls.'

'All I've said to the guv'nor was that there were one or two odd facts—'

'Facts are things which really exist, not wild dreams in what passes for a DC's mind. You can forget all that crap and do some work. Go down to Quince Street—'

'I'm getting some grub and then returning to the *Hakota* to have a look around the captain's cabin.'

'You're doing what I bloody well tell you.'

'Guv'nor's orders, sarge,' she said sweetly, enjoying the opportunity of being legitimately able to defy him.

Pickering, the relief third officer, looked into Dunn's cabin. 'You're in luck, chief!'

'What's caused so cosmic a shift in my affairs?'

'There's a smooth bit of skirt wants to chat with you.'

'Who is she?'

'A copper.'

'Detective Constable Ryan?'

'That's the bird.'

'Where is she?'

'On the main deck by the gangway.'

'It didn't occur to you to show her up?'

Pickering left. A young man far too pleased with himself, Dunn thought. He wearily pushed to one side of the desk the papers at which he was working. It would have helped if the captain had completed his work before falling on to the table. Dunn looked at his watch. A quarter to four. When at home, Estelle and he had had tea at four. She would make sandwiches, often with soft roes, and tell him she'd only have one because she mustn't gain another ounce, then would eat several. Strangely, she never gained weight, however much she ate . . .

Helen entered the cabin. 'Sorry about this, but they say a bad penny always comes back.'

He stood. 'Then it's a pity there aren't more bad pennies around! . . . You'd like to speak to more of the crew?'

'To have a look at the captain's accommodation.'

'For any particular reason?'

'To check up on one or two things before I make my report.'

Her tone had become curt. A warning that inquisitiveness

would not be welcome. 'I'll pick up the key from the chief steward, who's been holding it. Shan't be a moment.' He left.

She looked around herself. The cabin was small and made to seem smaller by the solid, clumsy furnishings in a very dark wood; little light came through the port because of its size and the overhang of the boat-deck. She would have been very unhappy to live in such surroundings – she liked space and light.

Dunn returned, led the way up to the captain's flat. He unlocked the door, pushed it open, gestured to her to enter. In the past, rank had unashamedly meant privilege. Both the day room and bedroom were very much larger and lighter than Dunn's cabin; beyond the bedroom, was a bathroom.

She visually examined the day room, then crossed to the table in the centre. The wood had been well scrubbed and showed no trace of blood. The metal brackets at each corner were solid and had definite edges, but she wondered if one of them could inflict as serious an injury as the photographs had shown. The forensic scientists could try to answer that one.

No attempt had been made to mask the safe, set in the far bulkhead. 'I'd like to see what's inside that,' she said, pointing.

'I don't know where the captain kept the keys.'

'If he was like almost everyone else, in the most obvious place. Try the desk.'

The two keys were in the top left-hand drawer. She unlocked the safe. Inside was a revolver, a box of bullets, files, loose papers, and a bundle of dollar notes secured with a rubber band. 'Is the revolver loaded?'

'I've no idea.'

'Is it usual for a captain to have a gun?'

'In this company, yes, because of the out-of-the-way places we call at. It's also handy to quell a mutiny.'

'That's likely?'

'If the meal's become even more inedible than usual.'

'Perhaps we should start thinking about mutinies at the station when the canteen assistant's doing the cooking,' she said lightly. 'What about all the files and papers – are they to do with ship's business?'

'The more confidential aspects of it, such as the captain's assessment of his officers, written on asbestos.'

'You don't seem to have liked Captain Sewell?'

'Occasionally, one respects one's captain. One never likes him.'

'Why's that?'

'He leads a solitary life and has no social contact with his officers since that's the only way of maintaining the myth of command. If a captain's manner is friendly rather than aloof, and he starts offering his officers drinks, you can guarantee he's a poor captain.'

'What kind of captain was Captain Sewell?'

'Bad on the human side – he could only criticize, never praise. But as a seaman, he was first-class.'

She reached into the safe and brought out the bundle of notes. 'Would this be the captain's money?'

'Almost certainly, the float.'

'What's that?'

'Dollars the captain holds for emergencies.'

'What kind of emergencies?'

'As I said, we sail to small, disorganized ports and quite often the docks and stevedores are run by local mafia. One of their favourite ploys is to threaten a strike which will leave the ship idle, but racking up the port dues. If a captain judges the delay is likely to be more costly to the company than the bribe, he pays up out of the float.'

'How much would be here?'

'I can't say. It'll be recorded on the appropriate form.'

'Which will be in the safe?'

'It should be.'

'Would you care to find it for me?'

He crossed to the safe, brought out files and loose papers, put them on the table and began to look through them. She picked up a file marked 'Officers' Assessments' and opened it. The top form, marked chief officer, had been filled in in spidery handwriting in pencil. The final judgment was that the chief officer was not suitable for promotion – the reasons for this made it clear it was the chief officer's manner which was held to be at fault, not his ability. A sharp clash of personalities, she decided. Not unknown in the police force.

'Here we are,' he said. 'On sailing from Coalpool, the float was five thousand dollars. Duly signed for by the old man.'

'Which old man?'

He smiled. 'The captain.'

'I'll check the amount.' She walked over to the safe.

'Is there a problem?'

'Why d'you ask?'

'What interests you doesn't on the face of it seem to have much connection with the accident.'

'We prefer to spend time covering all aspects of a case, even if some appear unimportant, rather than assume something is unimportant and later discover we were wrong.'

And politicians are honest, he thought.

'Where money is concerned, we always count it in front of a witness to make certain the sum's agreed. It's all too easy maliciously to accuse a police officer of theft.' She brought the notes out of the safe and put them down on the table, removed the rubber band. 'I'm going to have to be careful since the notes don't vary in size or colour – makes counting a bit tricky.'

'Have you been to America?'

'We were going just before Dean decided he—' She abruptly stopped speaking, counted rapidly. 'You said five thousand?'

'That's right.'

'I make it four thousand nine hundred and ninety-five dollars. Will you check, please?'

He did so. 'Four nine nine five, it is.'

'Then the captain had paid out five dollars?'

'I didn't think there was an entry to say he had. Hang on and I'll check.' He reread the float money form. 'There's no record of any withdrawal.'

'Perhaps the captain forgot to enter the five dollars.'

'Very unlikely.'

'Might he have borrowed them for his own use?'

'Even more unlikely.'

'Could the float have been five short at the beginning of the voyage?'

'He'd never have signed for it if it had been.'

'Then where do you suggest they might have gone?'

'I've no idea.'

She secured the notes with the rubber band. 'For the moment, it'll be best if everything is returned to the safe and you keep charge of the key.'

He gathered up the files, papers, and notes, stowed them in the safe, pocketed the key. He looked up at the clock on the bulkhead. 'It's just after five. The baker makes lousy bread, but great cakes, so would you like coffee?'

'Thanks, I would.'

They went below. Calvert, the officers' steward, was in the small pantry and Dunn spoke to him before following Helen into the smoke-room. They sat at one of the three tables.

'I suppose you'll soon be going on leave?' she said.

'Not for a while. The captain died when he was only halfway through the paperwork and I'm having to cope with it.'

'That's rotten luck for you and your family. Do you have children?'

'No.' Realizing how rudely abrupt he was sounding, he added: 'My wife preferred not to have any.'

'You say "preferred". Is she . . .' She stopped.

'Departed. But, as she made clear in her last letter, not dead.'

'I'm being impertinently inquisitive.'

He might not have heard her. 'She decided a fat bird in the bush was worth a thin one in the hand.'

Pickering entered the smoke-room. 'Hullo, again. Arresting the mate for impersonating an officer?' He laughed loudly, picked up a chair from the next table, sat down at theirs. 'So tell me something I've often wondered about – what's it like?'

'What is what like?' she asked coolly.

'Being a policeman?'

'I presume you mean, policewoman?'

Calvert, a tray in his hands, entered and crossed to their table, placed plates, saucers, and cups in front of Helen, sugar bowl, a jug of milk and a selection of small individual cakes on a plate between them.

'What about me, then?' Pickering asked.

'You want something?' Calvert spoke sourly.

'Too right. Coffee and three or four cakes, as quick as you like.'

Calvert left.

'Mind if I have one of yours whilst I'm waiting?' Pickering reached across and picked up an iced cake with crystallized cherry on top. 'I'm feeling right peckish. Didn't fancy the fish at lunch since it smelled of old socks and the beef was leather.' He picked off the cherry, held it between thumb and forefinger, spoke to Helen. 'I guess you've discovered what fun it is, popping the cherry.'

She ignored him.

'Have they discharged the middle 'tween at three yet?' Dunn asked sharply.

'I don't think so,' Pickering answered.

'Perhaps you'll make the effort to find out.'

'Sure.' He turned to Helen. 'I'll bet you like dancing.' He bit off a large part of the cake, spoke through the mouthful. 'They have old time dances at the local ballroom some nights. I've been told I'm a sharp dancer.'

'By a partner with a lacerated ankle?'

He laughed.

Calvert returned with a plate on which was a single individual cake.

'Where's the rest?' Pickering asked loudly.

'That's all that was left.'

'Then tell the baker to cook several more tomorrow. Where's the coffee?'

'Takes time to make.'

'Seems like you're growing the beans first.'

Calvert left.

'Do you enjoy the films?' Pickering asked Helen.

'Sometimes.'

'I've been told there's a blockbuster on at the moment that's well worth seeing. Maybe you'd like to find out if that's true?'

'I doubt we have the same tastes.'

'So let's find out.'

'I'm afraid I'm busy.'

'Doing what, I ask myself.'

'And no doubt provide an imaginative answer.' She spoke to Dunn. 'I'd better move.'

They left the smoke-room and went down the outside companionway to the main deck.

'I'm sorry about that,' he said, as they came to a halt by the gangway.

'About what?'

'Pickering's manner.'

'Just one more youth suffering from a surfeit of optimistic hormones,' she answered lightly and smiled. 'Thanks for all your help. And the cakes were every bit as delicious as you said they'd be.'

As she descended the gangway, he wondered if he shared her tastes in films.

Seven

'Take a seat,' Tait said.

Helen sat on one of the two chairs in front of the desk. It seemed the detective inspector was in one of his more pleasant moods.

'Tell me about your return visit to the boat.'

'The chief officer was very helpful and although I didn't learn anything of direct relevance, I'm thinking maybe I did turn up something of indirect relevance.'

'Which was what?'

She did not answer the question directly. 'Do you know Detective Chief Inspector Jones?'

'I've known two officers of that rank and name.'

'Toby Jones.'

'I've come across him.' Tait's tone was sharp. Toby Jones had been a DC when he'd been a DS. Another officer who had leap-frogged him in the promotion stakes.

'He was lecturing at the training college when I was there. He often said one of the basic arts of successful detection was the ability to sense a break in rhythm and go on to determine if it had any significance.'

He'd always been quick to underline the obvious.

'I came across a possible break on the *Hakota*.'

'Which was?'

She told him about the missing dollars.

'Easy enough to explain. The captain took the money out and forgot to record that fact at the time; he borrowed it for his own use and intended to repay it when back here, in England.'

'Mr Dunn was quite definite that the captain was too meticulous about observing rules to have forgotten, or to use the money privately.'

'Juniors often gain a wrong impression of their seniors.'

Had he the self-awareness to realize there might be a relevance to himself in that remark?

'Further, the missing money only begins to become a break in rhythm if one accepts without question the chief officer's judgment.'

'If the captain was struck on the head with something solid rather than falling on to the edge of the table, there's every chance there will be blood spatters.'

'You're now suggesting a forensic search?'

'Yes, sir.'

Tait rested his elbows on the desk, joined his fingers together, stared at her above his fingers. 'Presumably, you understand that will make another hole in our budget?'

'Not all that large a one.'

'There speaks someone who does not constantly risk heart failure through the stress of having to balance the books.' He looked past her at the far wall, his gaze unfocused, the sharpness of his features highlighted by the direction in which the light from the window met them. 'You suffer no doubts accepting the chief officer's opinion?'

'I don't think so.'

'I need a definite opinion.'

'I judge he was convinced the captain would never have removed five dollars from the float without recording that fact in writing.'

'Very well. I'll arrange for someone from SOCO to go aboard and check out the cabin.'

'Thank you, sir.'

'Keep your thanks until we know the result.'

* * *

Irwin parked the car, lifted the suitcase out of the boot, locked the car, and walked around the end of the cargo shed. He had expected to see a modern vessel, smartly painted; he saw an old, rusty freighter. Cranes were unloading three hatches; the ship's gear, the remaining three. Stevedores stowed the cargo in the shed, stealing what they could, when they could.

He came to a halt at the foot of the gangway and thought he should have been a mountaineer. Coalpool was a tidal port, the tide was in, the ship was riding high above the quay, the gangway rose at a steep angle, and his suitcase might not be large, but it was heavy.

He reached the deck short of breath and sweating; his wife constantly nagged him over eating too much, drinking too much, and smoking. He sought someone to direct him where to go, but the only persons visible were the hatchmen on the foredeck. There was a door in the accommodation and he opened this, stepped inside to meet a strange smell, neither sweet nor sour, neither pleasant nor unpleasant – ship's smell. To his left was a cabin and the door was open to show him that a man worked at the desk, a mass of papers before him. 'Can you tell me where I'll find the chief officer, Mr Dunn?' Irwin asked.

The chief steward looked round. 'Up top somewhere; maybe in his cabin,' he replied impatiently.

'How do I get to that?'

'The companionway at—'

'The what?'

'Stairs. Go up them and his cabin is for'd on the starboard side; if he's not there, try the captain's flat one deck up.'

The chief officer's cabin was shut and locked. Irwin climbed the second flight of stairs – to hell with sea lingo – and in the large room was a man in uniform, three gold bars on his sleeves, seated at a desk. 'Are you Mr Dunn?'

'I am.'

'PC Irwin.'

Dunn stood. 'Come on in.'

He entered and gratefully put down the suitcase.

'Is Detective Constable Ryan with you?'

'No. I'm from SOCO.'

'What does that mean?'

Irwin was gratified to be given the opportunity to expose someone else's ignorance. 'Scenes of crime officer.'

'Does . . . Wasn't the captain's death an accident?'

'I'm here to find out.'

So that explained why Helen had been interested in the money.

'This is the room he was found dead in?'

'Yes.'

'Can you tell me exactly where?'

'Some two feet aft of the port corner of the table.'

He thought he knew what that meant, so was damned if he was going to ask. 'I'm sorry to upset anything, but I'd like the place to myself.'

'I'll be grateful for the break. I'll be below if you want anything.' Dunn left.

Irwin visually examined the table, the deck, the bulkheads and the deckhead; he noted one very small, dark stain in the iron bracket at the corner of the table which had escaped being scrubbed away and identified it as dried blood – a test would have to confirm this since in court, white had to be proved to be white. He sprayed the bulkheads and the deckhead – this with difficulty and much cursing – with luminol, shone the beam of an ultraviolet torch over the surfaces. On the deckhead, a series of luminous stains became visible and these formed a pattern which had an unmistakable origin. Something solid had smashed into the captain's skull and as this had been jerked upwards after the blow, some of the blood on it had been scattered upwards by momentum.

He used the shore phone in the chief steward's cabin to call for a police photographer to come aboard.

Eight

'The guv'nor's been having a moan about you,' Marr said. 'And I can't blame him.'

That was a change, Helen thought.

'You've stuffed up the month's financial estimates.' Marr leaned back in his chair, used the fingers of his right hand to brush back his hair in an effort to hide the growing baldness, about which he was inordinately conscious. 'You'll never learn, will you?'

'Depends what the subject is.'

'You'll never learn not to brown-nose.'

'When the guv'nor asks me what's the score, I tell him.'

'You'll wear your nose right away.'

'Judge not from personal experience, that ye be not judged.'

'What the hell's that supposed to mean?'

'I'm not certain, but it sounds sufficiently portentous.'

'If you're trying to be insolent—'

'Perish the thought.'

About to speak angrily, he checked the words. Her self-confidence made him wary of her. Not that he would ever have admitted this. Women in the force were cannon-fodder. 'Do you know what I'd have said if you'd obeyed orders and reported to me first? I'd have said, you're talking little spherical objects.'

'Aren't they more elliptical?'

'The captain's float is missing five dollars. Common sense says he either helped himself or made a mistake counting. But you can't accept the obvious, can you? The five dollars must have been nicked by someone and that someone must have murdered the captain. A pity you didn't stop to ask yourself, where's the evidence he was murdered? No, you had to rush off to the DI and tell him you're so smart, you've worked out the captain was smacked on the head by the man who nicked the dollars. And the guv'nor was too polite to point out that only a half-wit would imagine a murderer would content himself with five dollars when there are five thousand staring at him.'

'I think he was caught when he was taking the money, which was why he had to murder the captain.'

'And having finished him off, why didn't he take the other four thousand, nine hundred and ninety-five?'

'Unnerved by what he'd done.'

'You unnerve me with your twisted imagination. Didn't that finishing school in Switzerland teach you any logic?'

'It wasn't a finishing school.'

'It certainly didn't finish you . . . Let me give you some advice. Carry on as you have been and it'll be a good idea to start wondering what you'd like to do in the outside world.'

Tait stepped into the room. Marr said: 'I've just been having a word with Constable Ryan, sir—'

Tait interrupted him. 'The preliminary report from SOCO on the captain's cabin has just come in.'

'And confirms there's no sensible reason to suspect anything but accident.'

'He was killed by a blow to the head delivered by a traditional blunt instrument.'

Marr's expression was one of resentful disbelief.

'We have a murder case on our hands. Something we just didn't need!'

'Can SOCO be that certain? They do make mistakes—'

'If you want to argue, do it with them.'

'Sir, there can't be an autopsy since the body was buried at sea—'

'They say the pattern of blood stains on the ceiling of the room is unmistakable.' He spoke to Helen. 'Good – if unwelcome – work on your part . . . When you were having a word with the crew, did you gain any suggestion of someone who hated the captain's guts?'

'No, sir. Although it was pretty obvious no one liked him.'

'What makes you say that?'

'More attitudes than actual words. Except the chief officer did say that no one ever likes a captain; at the very best, he's respected. I think Captain Sewell was respected as a seaman, not as a person.'

'Since you started this case running, you can continue with the preliminaries until the superintendent turns up to take command and decides who does what.' His tone had become sour. The detective superintendent was another contemporary. 'Begin the questioning of the crew. Do you know how many there are?'

'I don't, no.'

'Start with the officers since they'll have had far more contact with the captain.'

'Won't the crew be going on leave?'

'Shit! . . . We'll have to slow things down. Who do we speak to for that?'

'It'll be the marine superintendent,' Marr said quickly, eager to reassert himself.

'Then have a word with him.' Tait crossed to the door, stopped, turned back and spoke to Helen. 'Have you had any further thoughts about the five dollars?'

'As I said to Constable Ryan—' Marr began.

'I want her opinion, not yours.'

Helen said: 'I'm afraid I haven't come up with anything. Frankly, it doesn't seem to make any sense.'

'Unless the chief officer's judgment of the captain is wrong.'

'Which stands out a mile, it is,' Marr muttered.

Tait ignored him. He asked Helen: 'What kind of impression of Dunn have you gained?'

'A straightforward one so far, sir. I have learned one thing about him. When he was checking the contents of the safe, I had the chance to read the captain's confidential report on him. It was very critical and ended up saying Dunn was not suitable for promotion. But the way the whole report was phrased made me certain the criticisms were more the result of a conflict of character than comments on ability.'

'Find out how far that conflict extended. And read through all the rest of the confidential reports to find out if they offer any more information.'

'Yes, sir.'

He left the room, his stride brisk.

'I suppose you think you've been right smart?' Marr said sourly. 'Well, I'm telling you, you're just bloody lucky.'

As she left, she thought 'lucky' was not a word she would have used to describe herself. It was several months since Dean had told her he was breaking up their relationship because he'd met someone else, but she still felt emotionally bruised.

Captain Barton had been in command five years before being promoted (demoted?) to marine superintendent. He was short in stature and temper, had very light blue eyes, a hook nose, a thin-lipped mouth, and possessed a manner which he considered always reasonable, others, aggressively intolerant.

'You're telling me Captain Sewell was murdered?'

'Yes,' Helen answered.

'Christ!' He stared into space. 'Had a greaser on the *Returara* stab a deck-boy in the belly; took him four days to die. Nothing like this, of course.'

Because the severity of the crime depended on the rank

of the victim? 'We'll obviously be conducting an investigation, Captain Barton, and that means we'll need to question every member of the crew. So we're asking that for the moment, no one goes on leave.'

He glared at her. 'You realize what you're saying?'

'We'll do our best to make certain it is not for long.'

'And if you fail? Eventually, they'll have to go on leave because the law says they must and I'll have to find a full shore crew. What do you imagine management will say to me when they learn that?'

'I don't see how you can be blamed because they have to remain on it—'

He spoke angrily. 'Have you never learned a ship is always she? No idea why, of course.'

She was about to say, wearily, she had in fact recently learned why, but he forestalled her. 'Unless you keep a steady hand on her helm, she's all over the bloody place.' He waited for some reaction to what he'd said, was annoyed when she remained silent. 'I'll need the demand in writing and signed by someone considerably senior to you.'

She stood. 'Thank you for your help.'

He was further annoyed by her politeness.

She made her way down the ill-lit flight of stairs to the ground-floor office, which looked as if nothing had changed in many years, either to structure or staff. On her way to the outside door, she passed a glass case in which was a model cargo ship in the colours of the Akitoa Shipping Company. She was in perfect shipshape condition, superstructure and hull brightly painted and not a touch of rust. The image was always superior to the reality.

Tait swore as he replaced the receiver. He spoke to Helen, Marr, Yates and Wiseman, who were grouped around him in the CID common room. 'The super's arriving in half an hour, so I'm to remain here.' He turned to Marr. 'You're leading the team.'

'Then first I'll question the chief officer—'

'Helen can speak to him since she's already made contact.'

Marr's expression became sourer.

'The working premiss is that if theft had been the motive, either all or the majority of the dollars would have been stolen, so we need to consider alternatives. Personal relationships between captain and officers or members of the crew are important. Get moving and let's wrap this case up quickly.'

'I reckon one of us is going to strike lucky,' Pickering said, as he entered the chief officer's cabin. 'There's an army of police coming aboard and one of 'em's Helen. She may not be a raving beauty, but if you ask me, she'll make a first-class lay.'

'I didn't ask you.'

'You can always judge the potential from the way they walk. Move their hips just so and you can be certain they'll dance the tango at the moment critique.'

As Pickering left, Dunn looked down at the many-paged report on his desk. The quantities of perishable and dry stores remaining at the end of the previous voyage, consumed in port, loaded, consumed during the voyage, in hand. The figures had been drawn up by the chief steward and all he was now required to do was sign, as acting captain, his acceptance of their accuracy. Yet unless he had tallied in and out every pound of lamb, beef, pork, fish, fowl, butter, potatoes, flour, dried fruit, tea, coffee, tins of this and that, how in the hell could he? His signature was simply a rubber stamp unless or until the chief steward's depredations were uncovered, then it would be the means of loading blame on his shoulders.

There was a knock on the door and he looked round to see Helen in the doorway. He stood. 'You've arrived just in time for coffee and cakes.'

'Pure coincidence, on my honour.' She smiled.

Her face was redesigned by her smile, he thought once more. It filled her features with inner warmth. 'Have a seat and I'll go and organize things.'

'There's no call—'

'Speaking for myself, there's a great shout since I'm hungry and thirsty.'

Calvert was not in the pantry, so he went below to the crew's mess. Conversation had been loud before he entered; it abruptly stopped. The five men seated around the nearest table stared at him with the blank expression which hid the hostility rank provoked. He spoke to Calvert. 'Will you please bring coffee for two and some cakes up to my cabin?'

Calvert muttered something. In the company of his peers, he showed no deference to any officer.

'Yes.' Dunn left. As he reached the end of the alleyway, he heard ribald laughter. He could be certain he was the cause of that.

He entered his cabin. 'Refreshments should soon be here.' He sat, spoke slowly. 'Is it true Captain Sewell didn't die accidentally?'

'Yes, it is.'

'And you suspected that when you were last aboard?'

'I decided it was possible.'

He could remember her saying that all she was doing was checking facts for an accident report. Estelle had always been able to lie to him with complete success. When, for the umpteenth time, she'd told him she'd spent her time with Betty, he'd just been surprised they could find so much to talk about . . .

'I'm afraid I have to ask more questions.'

'Fire away.'

'The morning the captain was found dead in his cabin – where were you, what were you doing, what did you see and hear?'

'All that's in the report I gave you—'

'I know, but now we have to go through everything again and, if possible, in greater detail.

He spoke quietly, quickly. He'd arrived on the bridge at five minutes to four. The captain, exhausted because at his age a lack of sleep had a more adverse effect than on a younger man, had remained on the bridge until soon after six, when he had expressed a need to go below. The fog had thinned to the point there was no need to continue sounding the foghorn, so he had tried to speak to the captain over the voice pipe to ask permission to still it and when there was no reply, had assumed the other had fallen asleep. At eight, he had been relieved by the third officer; just after nine, when on breakfast relief, he had again tried to speak to the captain and, failing, had taken the wheel and sent the helmsman below to check if the captain was all right . . .

'You thought he might have been taken ill or suffered an accident?'

'Yes.'

'Yet earlier, you'd just assumed he'd fallen asleep.'

'I'd have expected that when I kept blowing, the whistle would have woken and alerted him, however deeply he'd been asleep. It would trigger a subconscious alarm.'

'Have you any idea who might have wanted to kill him?'

'None whatsoever.'

'You can't name anyone who clearly hated him, for whatever reason?'

'As I told you before, he wasn't liked or much respected, but that's a hell of a long way from the situation you're suggesting.'

'Why wasn't he respected?'

He had explained that to her as well. She probably remembered, but wanted to check his consistency of evidence. 'He was intolerant, often incapable of giving an order quietly and calmly, would not allow that something could go wrong through no one's fault, lost his temper over small things, damned, but never praised.'

'You're picturing someone who must have aroused sharp dislikes.'

'Inevitably, captains are autocrats. If their actions aroused murderous hatred, I don't suppose there'd be many left at sea.'

'You wouldn't imagine his manner of command was the motive for his murder?'

'I doubt the possibility.'

'How did you get on with him?'

'I survived.'

'Obviously. But how would you describe your relationship with him?'

'Fraught.'

'Can you be more explicit?'

'What more is there to say? Haven't you ever suffered a superior who picked out all your faults and was blind to any abilities?'

'A good question,' she answered, as she thought of Marr. 'So for you, dealing with the captain meant never explain, never complain?'

'Discipline with us isn't like it is with the services.'

'Are you saying you'd argue your case?'

'When necessary.'

'How did he react to argument?'

'With anger.'

'Was his relationship with the other officers similar?'

'In that one respect, he was an egalitarian.'

'Then isn't it reasonable to suppose someone did not accept his dictatorial manner in the same spirit as you did?'

'I thought I'd already answered that question.'

'I'm wondering if you were speaking instinctively, not after some deliberation.'

'I will now deliberate. The possibility the captain's style of command provoked someone into murdering him is ridiculous.'

'But he was murdered.'

'For some other reason.'

'Such as?'

'How would I know?'

Calvert, tray in one hand, knocked on the door and entered, put the tray down on the desk, left. There were five cakes. They each ate two.

Dunn picked up the plate and held it out. 'The last one gives you the choice between a thousand pounds and a handsome husband.'

'We have half each.'

'Five hundred pounds and half a husband?'

'I'll settle for the five hundred.'

'You already have a handsome husband?'

'No.' She picked up the knife from the tray, took the plate out of his hand, cut the remaining cake in half, chose the nearer piece, passed the plate back. 'I had a relationship which wasn't as solid as I'd thought. It's easy to deceive oneself.' She drank the last of the coffee, put the cup down on the saucer. 'I'd like to look through the confidential reports in the captain's safe.'

'I imagine I'm not allowed to ask why?'

'Correct.' She leavened her abrupt answer with a quick smile.

'His accommodation has been sealed by your people.'

'There'll be no need to reseal it. Is it all right to go upstairs now?'

It was his turn to smile. 'Up top.'

They made their way to the captain's flat. He broke the seal, unlocked the door and opened it, stepped to one side to let her enter first. He unlocked the safe, brought out the confidential reports and put them down on the desk. 'Do you want me standing by?'

'Have you something more important you'd like to do?'

'That has to be done, however reluctantly.'

'Then leave me here. Where will I find you when I've finished?'

'Almost certainly, in my cabin.'

He returned below, but did not immediately resume work. Pickering was right in one respect – she was no conventional beauty; yet when she smiled, she possessed an inner beauty . . . He finally picked up a pocket calculator and used it to confirm that the chief steward's calculations were correct. Mindless work, but were he to miss an error, however immaterial, shore office would enjoy giving him hell for signing an acceptance of the report.

He had just completed the work in which he was immediately employed when Helen returned. She stepped into the cabin. 'I've replaced everything in the safe, locked that, and here's the key.' She handed it to him. 'I'm keeping the room key for the moment.'

'Have you found anything? Or is that one more question which shouldn't be asked?'

'You're learning, if somewhat slowly! I'll leave you in peace and find out how the others are getting on. Many thanks for the hospitality and you'll be glad to know I'll try to make certain that if I have to return, it won't be at coffee time.'

'Sorry to hear you say that . . . I've been thinking. From one or two of the things you've said, I gather we're maybe in the same boat. Is that right?'

'All the time I'm aboard, that surely has to be so?'

'We've both been left footloose. So I'm wondering if we could find a film that would be to your taste and have a meal afterwards?'

'That's kind, but I'm afraid I'm very busy at the moment.'

'A pity.'

'Yes, it is. Goodbye.' She walked up the cross-alley, turned left to go out of his sight.

He sat. Was she too busy to enjoy an evening with him? She had said she had been in a relationship which had clearly turned sour; perhaps she could have added that she'd formed another which hope decided would be much longer lasting.

Pickering stopped outside the open doorway and looked into the cabin. 'Did she come and have a chat with you?'

'Yes.'

'And?'

'She asked questions, I answered them.'

'And when she'd finished, how did she answer your question?'

'She left.'

'Bad luck. But one can't win them all. And likely she's waiting for me to ask.'

Nine

In the force, Detective Superintendent Campbell was known as the Bulldog. His face was heavily jowled, his manner aggressive, and his bite was worse than his bark. He was thirty pounds overweight, because his wife was a very good cook, intelligent, possessed of considerable common sense, had a quick temper, and was intolerant of slackness.

He sat at the window-end of the table in the conference room. Tait – looking sullenly resentful because Campbell was no diplomat and had taken command of the case with curt authority – Marr, Yates, Wiseman, Horne, and Helen were on either side of it. In front of him were several files and loose papers, but he seldom consulted them, having a sharp memory. His voice was deep, his Rs slightly confused. 'Each of you can give me a brief résumé of what you've learned so far, starting with you.' He looked at Wiseman, on his immediate left.

Wiseman reported he had spoken to Tucker, who, being the captain's steward, was almost certainly in the best position to provide information about the dead man. He'd kept the questioning very low key, making it more a friendly chat than—

'Get on with it,' Campbell snapped.

Tucker had found it difficult to describe his relationship with the captain. Captains did not become friendly with their tigers. Captain Sewell had had a quick temper and had always created hell when something was not to his liking.

But what officer didn't take his anger out on someone else? Normally, the captain had said very little other than to give an order. His wife, who had once come aboard when they were in port, looked as if she dined on ice—

'Never mind the wife. Did he hear the captain rowing with officers or crew?'

The captain criticized his officers all the time. The second and third just remained quiet, but the chief officer often argued back, much to the captain's fury.

Campbell, who'd been making notes with a ball-point pen which only functioned fitfully, making him swear, looked up. 'Did you ask about any particularly fierce row?'

'He was mostly vague about details, but there was an incident on the last voyage he remembered quite clearly. The captain asked the chief officer why a rat's-tail hadn't been cleared—'

'What's that?'

'I gather it's a loose bit of string or material that's caught up on a rope or wire and is flapping in the wind. The chief officer said he'd been too busy organizing the freeing of an engine-room ventilator to worry about it. The captain told him he was so slack, he wasn't fit to crew a Thames barge; the chief officer replied with words to the effect that at least the barge would be skippered by someone who knew how to command. Tucker said he thought the captain would have a stroke, he was so furious.'

'Small wonder the captain's confidential report on the chief officer was critical. Did Tucker have any more information?'

'He mentioned Grainger, a stoker. On the previous trip, when the ship was in Geelong, Grainger brought a couple of tarts aboard late at night. The captain saw them and had the two women thrown off the ship and logged Grainger.'

'It was against the rules to have women aboard?'

'It was left to the captain's discretion and, according to Tucker, Sewell was a Holy Joe about it. This last trip,

Grainger was still cursing the captain for making him pay twice for nothing.'

'Who questioned Grainger?'

'I did, sir,' Horne replied.

'What's he have to say about this incident?'

'I didn't know about it.'

Campbell spoke to Tait. 'You don't believe in team work?'

'I can hardly be expected to—'

'Question him,' Campbell ordered Horne, 'and determine how relevant it is.' He asked Marr for his report.

'I spoke to the second and third officers, sir, since it was obvious that they were the most likely to be able to give us relevant information.'

'And did they?' Campbell snapped, his tone expressing his dislike of someone who sought to ingratiate himself by stressing his own importance.

'Not really, no.'

'Are we going to hear what they did say?'

'The second officer was on the bridge from midnight to four. The fog was still thick and the captain was on the bridge throughout. When I asked him how the captain had appeared to be, his reply was, the usual bad-tempered bastard. It seemed to me from the way he spoke that something might have occurred, so I asked what had happened. The captain wouldn't allow smoking on the bridge, so the second officer had climbed up to the monkey island to have a cigarette. The captain caught sight of the flare of the match and gave the second hell for disobeying orders and told him he wasn't fit to man a barge.'

'The captain seems to have had a thing about barges,' Campbell said dryly.

Marr waited, continued speaking. 'At four, the chief officer relieved him and he went down to his bed and that's all he can tell. I asked him about the captain and he again said he was an ill-tempered bastard who never stopped finding fault, so it wasn't surprising someone had murdered him, but he'd no idea who that was.

'He very obviously disliked the captain and, in my opinion, was a bit scared of him.'

Campbell picked up his pen and began to fiddle with it. 'Has any of you wondered why the officers are serving on the ship?'

No one answered.

'It's an old bucket that should have been sent to the scrapyard years ago. Why are they on her instead of a modern ship run by a decent company?'

Once again, there was no answer.

'One possibility is because they can't find a better berth. So check if that is so; and if it is, why. As quick as you like, to make up for lost time.'

Tait's lips tightened. There was no missing the inference he should have considered the question before.

Campbell spoke to Marr. 'You interviewed the third officer – what's his name?'

'Moran, sir.'

'What could he tell you?'

'He was on the bridge from eight until midnight. Describes the captain as always bad tempered. And out of touch. The officers had to wear uniform on the bridge and weren't allowed to smoke. They all had to take noon sights and write out the ship's position and average speed on a piece of paper and take it to him. Said it was like being back at school.'

'He resented all that?'

'And also found it stupidly funny. Even funnier was the way the captain made out he was so high-minded he wouldn't allow tarts aboard to cheer up the crew. Yet when he had the chance and no one would know about it, he dipped his wick smartly.'

'Supposition, wishful slander, or fact?'

'When the ship was in Porto Cavado, the third was in

the Gut – just passing through to somewhere else according to him – and he saw the captain.'

'What's the Gut?'

'The red-light area. To quote the third, imagination there will never catch up with fact.'

'That shows the captain had a human side, but not much else. What did Moran say about his relations with the other officers and crew?'

'Said no one liked the man, but he couldn't name anyone who hated him so much he'd have killed him.'

'Does he admit to rows with the captain?'

'If one didn't argue with him, said yes, sir, no, sir, things weren't all that difficult. Moran's the kind of bloke who bows his shoulders at trouble.'

Campbell turned to Helen. 'What about the chief officer?'

'Sir, I'd like to say something.'

'You can hardly answer without saying something.'

'Sergeant Marr has just mentioned the captain being in the Gut. Why was he there?'

'Do I need to explain certain facts of life to you?'

Marr sniggered.

'Do you know Chief Inspector Jones, sir; Toby Jones?'

'Yes.'

'He often said that if there was a break in rhythm, it was important to find out why.'

'Not again!' Marr muttered.

'What's that?' Campbell demanded.

'Nothing, sir.'

'Carry on, Ryan.'

'We've heard the captain was considered a Holy Joe; that he wouldn't allow women aboard and when he saw the stoker with two, he made certain they went straight back ashore. That suggests someone who held very old-fashioned standards and was sufficiently prejudiced he was determined to make others do the same. Yet he was in the Gut. There's a break in rhythm here.'

'Only if you assume he wasn't a total hypocrite.'

'My reading is, he was too sternly straightforward and inflexible to be a hypocrite . . . I think it would be worth making some enquiries.'

'On what grounds?'

'Suppose he wasn't in the Gut for sex?'

'Suppose politicians are honest!' Marr said.

Campbell said: 'You don't agree there could be reason to make enquiries?'

'No, sir,' Marr answered, believing Campbell was of the same opinion as he.

Cambell spoke to Tait. 'Your opinion?'

'Constable Ryan initially claimed there was a break in the rhythm of the case and that's why we're here.'

Campbell drew a lopsided circle on paper in front of him. 'Red-light areas spawn crime. So if the captain wasn't after sex, he was pursuing something else. What?'

No one answered.

'Tait, contact the police in Porto Cavado to find out if they can offer any help. Is the place a centre for any particular criminal practice, most especially one which would interest the captain of a tramp . . . Ryan have you anything more to add?'

'No, sir,' Helen answered.

'Then what can you tell us about the chief officer?'

'I questioned him yesterday afternoon. I can't say I learned anything fresh . . . He disliked the captain, but for my money there's no suggestion dislike turned into murderous hatred. In fact, I'd say there was more contempt than anything.

'He went on watch at four in the morning, relieving the second officer. The captain was on the bridge. Soon after the steward brought up tea and sandwiches – which makes it around six – the captain said he had to go below. Later, with the fog lifting, Dunn decided the foghorn could be turned off, but because he had to have the captain's agreement, he tried to contact him over the voice pipe. There was no answer. He presumed that the captain, having been up all night, had fallen asleep. He was relieved by the third officer at eight o'clock. After breakfast, in turn he relieved the third officer for his meal. He again tried to contact the captain, this time at length, but failed. He told Varley, the man who was steering, to go down and see if the captain was all right. Dunn took the wheel. Varley returned to say the captain was lying on the floor and looked dead.'

'Who else was on the bridge around six o'clock?'

'No one. That is, except for the stand-by when he brought up tea and sandwiches.'

'Would the man steering always know where the officer on duty was?'

'I can't answer that.'

'We need to know . . . How do you find Dunn as a man?'

'Pleasant, friendly, self-confident.'

'Is he married?'

'I gather his wife's deserted him. He hasn't any children.'

'How friendly?'

She smiled briefly. 'To the extent that he offered me coffee and cakes. And the cakes were the best I've eaten in a month of Sundays.'

'Have you anything more to add?'

'No, sir.'

'Who questioned members of the crew?'

Horne and Yates indicated they had.

'You first,' he said to Horne.

Horne's report was brief. The bosun, carpenter, and lamptrimmer had been turned in on the night of the murder. The captain's manner of command lost him respect, but all three thought it ridiculous to suppose he'd ever given someone cause to murder him. Sure, there were those who had talked wildly after receiving one of his verbal assaults – Grainger was one of them – but meaningless nonsense was spoken in every seamen's mess. As to the officers – the mate was a seaman, the second not half as smart as he thought himself, the third didn't like work.

Yates's evidence was no more positive. None of the other deck crew or engine-room staff could offer information of any real significance.

Campbell began to collect up his files and papers, which during the course of the meeting had become spread about the table in front of him. 'I want details of the officers' histories and a request sent to the police in Porto Cavado for any information they can give us. Has anyone any further suggestions? . . . No?' He turned to Helen. 'No further reaches of the imagination?' His tone was light.

'No, sir.'

He stood. 'I presume an office has been made ready for me?'

'Not yet, sir,' Tait said. 'We're having to move a load of records and junk out of it.'

'Then I'll use your room.'

Tait's expression signalled four-letter words.

They left the conference room and returned upstairs. Marr came to a halt in front of his room and waited for Helen to draw level with him, said: 'Are you sure you know what a man needs when he goes looking for a whore?'

She walked on.

Ten

Pickering entered the smoke room, crossed to the nearest table, and poured himself a cup of coffee. 'I'll be off in half an hour.'

'Off where?' Dunn asked.

He picked up a cake and took a large bite out of it, spooned sugar into a mug of coffee, initially spoke through a mouthful. 'The marine super said none of you were getting any leave until things are sorted out, so there's no call for me to relieve anyone. I'm being transferred to the *Ranaka*; but she's not due in until next week, so being owed some leave, I'm off home.' He put the rest of the cake into his mouth, picked up the last one on the plate, carried it in one hand, the mug in the other, to one of the chairs. 'My second best girlfriend is going to have a great surprise when I turn up unexpectedly.'

He was far too self-centred to consider the possibility it might be he who would have a great surprise, Dunn thought. 'Why isn't your best girlfriend also going to be delighted?'

'She's gone off to Holland for a fortnight.' He put the rest of the first cake in his mouth and ate before he said: 'Ever been to Amsterdam?'

'No.'

'Went there with a mate a couple of years back. We had a walk down that street to look at all the tarts on show in the windows.'

'You surprise me.'

Pickering loudly drank some coffee, finished the second cake. 'Who do you think did it?'

'Did what?'

'Knocked the old man on the head.'

'I've no idea.'

'I gather he was a real bastard.'

'I can only attest as to his figurative persona.'

'What are you on about?'

Dunn didn't answer.

'Is it straight that he acted like he was on a cruise ship and wanted the officer on watch in uniform even at night?'

'It is.'

'Bloody ridiculous in a company like this one.'

'He was a true seaman which compensated for the quirks.'

'Not for me, it wouldn't.' Pickering stood. 'I'll be on my way, then.'

'Good luck.'

'No worry on that score. Jeanie likes it as much as me.' He left.

Dunn wondered if Cedric boasted how Estelle . . . He forced his mind away from a question as pointless as it was painful. Yet again, he wondered what to do when he finally went on leave. Ask his cousin if he could stay with her? He got on well with her husband, and their two daughters were more fun than trouble, but Elisabeth was an emotional woman and would express her sympathy for him to the extent it would hurt rather than console. Stay in the Lake District and hope to find the peace and inner contentment he'd once known there? . . . He had never thought he could be depressed by the question of leave.

He made his way to his cabin, sat, ignored the diminishing pile of files and papers, and stared at the far bulkhead. He'd instinctively liked Helen when they'd met. A liking reinforced by their further meetings. Because a liking was usually reciprocated, because she had not mentioned a firm relationship, he had hoped she would accept his invitation. She had turned it down. Too busy. A traditional way of avoiding further contact.

The shore foreman looked into his cabin. 'There you are, chief.'

He silently agreed, there he was. 'A problem?'

'How did you guess? The port winch at number one has packed up again.'

'That's becoming a habit.'

'It's a wonder any of 'em work. Out of the Ark.'

'At least they're not steam. OK, I'll find the duty electrician and ask him to fix it.'

'As quick as you like since there's not a crane to take over.' He left.

Dunn stood. The broken winch might have halted the discharge of cargo at number one hatch, but its immobility was of some benefit – it provided him with a problem to occupy his mind.

'I won't bother you for long,' Helen said.

'That's right,' Captain Barton said loudly, 'you won't.'

She wondered why his mother had not had something done to his nose when he was young?

'Well, what do you want this time?'

'Do you mind if I sit?'

'If you must.'

She settled on the chair in front of the desk. 'I'm afraid I'm going to have to be frank.'

'That'll make you a unique female.'

She smiled, hoping to lessen his antagonism. 'The *Hakota* is an old boat, isn't she?' She prided herself on remembering that boats were feminine.

'Ship, woman, ship.'

The sea provided an ocean of solecisms. 'And the Akitoa Shipping Company isn't exactly Cunard. So it's probable a first-class officer wouldn't normally serve in it?'

'How many more goddamn insolent questions have you got?'

'I said I'd have to be blunt.'

'This is a tramp company. There's no money in tramping and never has been. It's run on a shoestring and the crew are what we can get.'

'So some of the officers are unqualified?'

'You think we'd send our ships to sea with officers who didn't have the certificates their ranks demand?'

'But there are better jobs going?'

'When aren't there, unless you're in the bloody EU parliament?'

'What can you tell me about the officers of the *Hakota*?'

'Why should I tell you anything?'

'Because this is a murder inquiry and we need certain information. We prefer it to be given voluntarily.'

He stared at her for several seconds, stood and left the room, returned with a folder in his hands. He sat, opened the folder, sorted through several papers, looked up. 'Dunn, the chief officer, came to us from the Beltrane Line.'

'I seem to know the name. Don't they do cruises?'

'No. They have a fleet of container ships.'

'Is it a good company?'

'What's your idea of "good"? The opposite of this outfit? The Beltrane Line was started in windjammer days and sailed some of the finest clippers to China. Nowadays, their ships run to Australia, New Zealand, Japan, and the west coast of the States.'

'It's an important company?'

'Very much so.'

'Why would Dunn have left it?'

'Isn't that obvious?'

'Not really.'

'He was slung out.'

'You know that for fact?'

'I use my common sense.'

'Why might he have been dismissed?'

'Drunkenness, theft, insubordination, screwing the chairman's wife . . . Try your imagination for further suggestions.'

'Didn't you ask him why he left them?'

'It's not my job to hire or fire.'

'Wouldn't whoever was responsible have questioned him and checked with someone in the Beltrane Line to find out why he had left them?'

'You think we'd get a straight answer? Make accusations and the lawyers hover around like bleeding vultures. An innocuous reference leaving out the black bits avoids that.'

'Can you tell me anything more about his past than you have?'

'No.'

'What about the other officers?'

He quickly read through papers in the file. 'Both Moran and Lewis came from the Atlantic and Pacific Steamship Company.'

'What kind of concern is that?'

'It isn't. Went bilges up financially a few years back.'

'Then they weren't thrown out?'

'Depends what you call redundancy.'

'Why didn't they try to get into a bigger company than this one?'

'They likely did, but there are fewer ships at sea and so there are fewer berths, many of which go to foreigners. And if you've a wide choice, you don't choose either of them.'

'Why not?'

'The only thing which makes them seamen is their mates' tickets.'

'There's only one more question. Where are the Beltrane offices?'

'Gower Street.'

'Thanks.' She closed her notebook.

'Are you thinking one of 'em killed the captain?' he asked.

'No.'

'So why ask questions of no bloody relevance?'

'That's my job.'

'The job of half the population these days.'

She thanked him for his help, said goodbye, left. After a brisk walk, she turned into Gower Street, which offered a sharp difference from where she'd been twenty minutes before. Here, there was little evidence Coalpool was a port town; no ships' chandlers, grotty bars, cheapjack shops, and waiting women. The buildings, a few of which were half-timbered, were untouched by grime or neglect, shops sold upmarket goods, pedestrians were reasonably dressed. An even greater contrast was provided by Beltrane Line's offices. Behind the show window was a beautifully presented model of a large ship, her deck laden with containers, and ranged on either side of her in a semicircle were framed photographs of ports to which the company's ships sailed.

Helen went in and spoke to a young woman, who asked her to wait while she had a word with Mr Abbott. Three minutes later, she directed Helen through the doorway at the far end and up the stairs to the first floor, where she would be met.

Abbott was tall, well built, handsome, dressed with care; he projected a warm, attentive personality. She was prepared to dislike him, always distrusting perfection.

'If you would like to come this way, Miss Ryan . . . Or should I be awarding you your rank?'

'As you like.'

'You'll be Miss Ryan. So much more companionable.'

She wondered how long he spent each morning admiring his reflection in the mirror.

The office was large and furnished with tasteful expense. He held an easy chair for her to sit, then went round the large partner's desk and settled. 'I must confess I am curious to know how I may be able to assist the police.'

His smile was broad, but his deep blue eyes were sharp. Not as lightweight as he appeared, she judged. 'Have you heard that the captain of the *Hakota* was killed when the ship was at sea?'

'I was told that, but thought it was the usual nonsense and he probably died from natural causes. But you're telling me that it was fact?'

'Yes.'

'And you are here because of that? Then I still have to wonder how I, or anyone else in the company, can help you in your enquiries.'

'By saying under what circumstances Felix Dunn left this company.'

He said: 'That is a strange request.'

'But pertinent.'

'Not impertinent?' He chuckled.

'I'd be grateful for an answer.'

'Unfortunately, I am unable to earn your gratitude. That sort of detail is not in my province.'

'Then perhaps you'll have a word with someone in whose province it is?'

He stood. 'Will you be kind enough to excuse me for a moment?'

She nodded.

'Most kind,' he murmured. He left.

She looked more closely about herself. Even the superintendent's office at divisional HQ was almost a slum compared to this room. How many years of her salary had the furnishings cost?

He returned, sat. 'I've had a word with a colleague and he has confirmed that unfortunately we are unable to answer you.'

'Why's that?'

'We do not have the information.'

'It must be in the records.'

'As I'm sure you'll know from your job, the problem of safe storage of records is a never-ending one, despite all the modern technology. Consequently, we do not keep information after a certain period if it is not important and the reason for the departure of an officer normally has to be of little relevance.'

He was lying. Guarding the company's back. 'I've been told this is one of the top shipping companies,' she said.

'You will not expect me to deny that.'

'And officers are very keen to serve on its ships.'

'I don't consider it an exaggeration to say an officer will consider he has reached the pinnacle of his profession when he joins us.'

'So few will ever willingly leave you?'

'Before retirement, certainly not.'

'Then for an officer to leave as Mr Dunn did, just over three years ago, must be very unusual. So someone working here will almost certainly remember the circumstances of his leaving.'

'I rather doubt that.'

'Why?'

'It was of small consequence and three years is a long time.'

'It was of great consequence to Mr Dunn.'

'I was speaking from the company's point of view.'

'Unusual occurrences stay in the memory.'

He smiled his disagreement.

'It is important to us to know why he left.'

'I can only express my regret at not being able to help you answer the question.'

'If you're afraid of laying the company open to legal action, I can assure you that everything you say to me now is in the strictest confidence.'

'I can only repeat what I have just said.'

'Then we may well have to return and question the staff at some length.'

'You will, of course, do whatever you find it necessary to do.'

It was like trying to stab a blob of mercury. She stood. He immediately did the same. 'Thanks for all your help,' she said sarcastically.

'It is a person's duty to give the police all the aid he can. If I may be so frank, you have made it a pleasure as well as a duty.'

If she had had a custard pie in her hands, she would have thrown it.

'Let me escort you out.'

She was surprised and a little disappointed that he did not bow when he said goodbye.

Eleven

In the commandeered DI's room, Campbell had taken off his coat and hung it on the back of the chair; he was wearing braces coloured red, white, and blue. They reminded Helen of a clown in one of the pantomimes to which she and Dean had gone after he had decided to write a book on the history and art of the English pantomime. His intentions had always been more active than his performances . . .

'Do you intend to spend the next half hour staring into space?' he demanded.

'Sorry, sir.'

'What have you learned?'

'The marine superintendent—'

'Sit down, woman, unless you prefer standing.'

Campbell might have had a rumbustious character, often objectionably so, but he did not force rank as some did. She sat. 'Captain Barton had no hard information, but since the Beltrane Line is a very prestigious company, it seems certain Dunn did not voluntarily leave them. He was probably sacked.'

'Barton couldn't say what for?'

'He suggested drunkenness, theft, enjoying the favours of the chairman's wife, or anything else I cared to imagine.'

'The only chairman's wife I've ever met would have to demand the favour in order to be granted it.'

'I went on to the offices of the Beltrane Line and spoke

to a Mr Abbott, who told me that because of the pressure of space, the company doesn't keep records concerning minor matters and the reason for Dunn's departure is, for them, a minor matter.'

'This in the days of hard disks?'

'Quite. What concerned him was covering the company from any possible trouble.'

Campbell picked up a pack of cigarettes, offered it, took out a cigarette and lit it. 'My wife keeps on at me to give up smoking, so I have to do it all away from home.' He leaned back in the chair and stared at the ceiling.

So do you intend to spend the next half hour staring up at heaven? she wanted to ask.

'Do we put pressure on this Abbott to give us some facts?'

'I'd say he's too slippery. He's PR marked all over him. And how do we prove they're lying when they say they don't keep the records we want?'

'How indeed? . . . OK.'

She accepted that as dismissal and left.

Yates was the only DC in the general room. 'So how are things going?' he asked, as she crossed to her desk.

'Not very smoothly.'

'Then you need a hand.'

'But not one of yours.' She sat.

'I've been thinking about you.'

'Curb your optimism.'

'You've been looking tired and troubled. You know what would make you feel rejuvenated?'

'Don't bother to offer me Viagra.'

'A night of good food, fun, and careless rapture.'

'Hamburgers and wrestling on the sofa with fumbling fingers? I'd rather watch the telly.'

'A meal at the Italian restaurant in Almart Street, a visit to the new disco, and a drive to Start Point with a full moon covering everything in lemon silver. It would make a new woman of you.'

'Who'd still say no.'

'You're hard.'

'Which is more than you're going to be where I'm concerned.'

'You don't recognize honest admiration.'

'I understand dishonest ambition.'

Marr stepped into the room, addressed Helen. 'Where have you been all morning?'

'Questioning Captain Barton, the marine superintendent, and Abbott at the Beltrane Line's offices.'

'Why?'

'Because the super told me to.'

'It never occurred to you to enter that information in the Movements Book? How the bloody hell can I run CID if I don't know where people are or what they're doing?'

She remembered she'd been about to make the entry in the Movements Book – recording the time she left divisional HQ and the reason for her absence – but at the last moment, something had distracted her.

'You think you don't need to be bothered with the rules?'

He hadn't added, 'Because you are a woman,' but the words were there, even if silent.

'If you don't want a flimsy in red, you'd better pull your act together.'

If he were left to write her flimsy – the biannual report on which an officer's career rested – she would definitely need to look for a new job.

Marr turned and left.

'I didn't think it possible until now,' Yates said, 'but he is becoming ever more objectionable. The guv'nor is in a foul mood because the super has taken over the case, so he takes it out on the sarge; the sarge gets rid of his resentment by giving us hell; so how do we relieve ourselves?'

'Differently.'

He laughed. 'You've a quick tongue.'

Only because she'd have led a miserable life at work if she didn't.

Campbell crossed to the window of the conference room and stared out at the rain which had been falling for half an hour, greying the scene. Tait and Marr sat at the table.

'We're getting nowhere fast,' Campbell finally said. He turned, crossed to the chair at the head of the table and sat. 'We've learned nothing from the crew, forensics say they can't give us any more because there's no body, and any lead we try to follow up ends dead. We have to start rethinking.' He brought a pack of cigarettes out of his coat pocket and offered it; Tait refused, Marr accepted and hastened to strike a match for them. 'Motive and opportunity usually help identify chummy, but not this time since we have uncovered no obvious and strong motive and in theory almost anyone aboard could have gone to the captain's cabin between the relevant times. So we're going to have to start relying on intuition. Tait – who is the prime suspect?'

'One of the officers or Tucker, the captain's steward.'

'Why Tucker?'

'He was in constant contact with the captain and although he denies knowing where the safe keys were, it's odds on he did.'

'You're suggesting theft was the motive when only five dollars were stolen out of the five thousand?'

'Murder has been carried out for less, sir. And I get the impression he's on the defensive.'

'Have his statements been thoroughly cross-checked?'

'He shares a cabin with Grose, who alibis him throughout the possible times of the captain's death.'

'Marr?'

'I agree with the inspector, sir. Tucker is rather too helpful, too eager to tell us how everything was. Of course, that could be his normal manner or he has a guilty conscience because of trying to bring in a few bottles of booze and he thinks helping us will put us off suspecting him of smuggling.' His tone became ingratiating. 'But like you so rightly said, sir, is he going to commit murder for five dollars?'

'And as the inspector pointed out, murder has been committed for less.' Campbell's tone was sharp, expressing his dislike for someone who tried to please him. 'What about the officers?'

'We've uncovered no motive other than resentment at the captain's manner of command,' Tait answered.

'Which hardly makes a motive. Are any of them alibied?'

'The second and third officers claim to have been asleep in their cabins; no one can confirm that. On the face of things, the chief officer has a solid alibi because he was on the bridge, but I questioned the two men who were steering the ship, one from four to six, the other from six to eight, and both agreed that when an officer has gone out of the wheelhouse on to the wing, they could not normally be certain he was still there.'

Campbell began to tap on the table with the fingers of his right hand. 'Murder was uncovered because Constable Ryan remembered to look for a break in rhythm. Since we're not getting anywhere, we'll do that now.'

Marr silently swore, accepting it was illogical to resent the decision, yet remembering what he had said to Helen.

'What have we learned that is out of rhythm? Possibly the captain's visit to the Gut. What that signifies, if anything, there's no way of knowing until the police in Porta Cavado can be bothered to reply. There's the fact Dunn, said by more than one to be a first-class officer – and in my book, ambitious – should leave a top company and come to this outfit, which must be as downmarket as you can get. Ryan asked Captain Barton if he knew why Dunn had quit the Beltrane Line; he would do no more than suggest possibilities. She then questioned Abbott in the Beltrane offices and he claimed no records of unimportant matters were kept for long because of storage space. We can assume that is balls, so, Tait, you go along, use your weight, and demand the truth.'

'It'll maybe have to wait until Monday, sir. Shore staff likely don't work over the weekend.'

'Don't take that for granted in order to skive off and enjoy a round of golf.'

'I don't play golf,' Tait replied resentfully, missing the intended humour.

'Marr, question Tucker with plenty of heat. Make it obvious you're curious and maybe about to become suspicious.'

'Yes, sir.'

'Then that's about it for the moment.'

Tait and Marr stood and were about to cross to the door when Campbell's comment stopped them. 'I don't intend this to become another unsolved case, so for once pull both fingers out.'

If the form of command could become the motive for murder, Tait thought, Campbell might well become a victim.

Moran entered the smoke-room and spoke to Dunn, the only other person present. 'Have you seen Brian, Chief?'

'Not since breakfast.'

'Where the hell's he got to? We're supposed to be going ashore for lunch.'

'Sounds as if you're assuming I'm remaining aboard on shore watch.'

'But . . . Didn't he clear that with you?'

'He did not.'

'I thought he'd spoken to you and you'd said you didn't mind remaining aboard.'

'The illogical optimist, par excellence.'

'Does that . . . Chief, have you plans ashore?'

'For lunch, no.'

'Then do you think you could stay aboard?'

'OK. But only for the afternoon.'

'Great! Can't tell you how grateful . . . Going out tonight?'

'Maybe.'

'One of us will make certain to be back in good time. It'll likely be me if the waitress turns out to be blonde, under sixty, and listens to Brian's blarney.' He left.

Dunn wondered why he had said he might go ashore. On a Saturday night, Coalpool had little to offer him. There were discos, many restaurants, one or two of which did not serve overpriced food, films, probably a concert at Trighley Hall, greyhound racing, but such pleasures were for two, not one; there were the tarts who walked the roads south of High Street, but he'd never bought temporary pleasure because of an old-fashioned fear of disease – one of his cousins was a specialist in venereal diseases and seemed to believe everyone was as interested in his speciality as himself.

When on leave, on a Saturday night, Estelle and he had often . . . He silently swore. Could his mind never forget the past? If he had Helen's phone number, if she had been at home and not out with a boyfriend, if she had not said she was too busy . . . If ifs and ands were pots and pans . . .

Twelve

The fax arrived at 1250hrs on Monday morning. The civilian secretary collected up the two sheets of closely printed A4 and carried them up to Tait's office. The door was partially open, so she knocked and went in, was surprised to see Campbell seated behind the desk.

'Yes?' Campbell said.

'I'm looking for Inspector Tait.'

'Why?'

She was tempted to answer it was none of his business, but there was a hint in Campbell's manner to suggest he was not a good man to challenge. 'There's a fax for him.'

'Who from?'

'Someone called Inspector Oldemiro Manjate,' she answered, having trouble in pronouncing the names.

'You can give it to me.'

She hesitated.

'Good God, it won't be some female propositioning the inspector.'

Expressing her silent disapproval, she put the pages down on the desk, left.

Women delighted in taking offence for absurd reasons, he thought, as he picked up the fax and read. He expressed his surprise aloud in terms he would have been loath to have carried out. He used the internal phone to call Tait to the room.

Tait entered and was annoyed to note some of the books in the bookcase had been moved; a man of precision, he always had them lined up exactly as he wanted. When a guest in someone's house, did the superintendent rearrange the bedroom?

'This has just come through.' Campbell pushed the pages across the desk. 'It's in a kind of English.'

Tait picked up the fax and read, transferring his weight from one leg to the other as he did so – he suffered from back pain. The chief of police in Porto Cavado sent his best wishes to the honoured and esteemed Superintendent Campbell. Every effort had been made to answer his questions, but all enquiries had failed until Guilherne Mocumbi was arrested for killing his companion with a knife after a drunken brawl. A man with many arrests and convictions, he was afraid he would suffer the maximum penalty for his crime and in order to try to lessen his punishment, had hinted he could tell the police something interesting about an English captain provided it was to his benefit to do so. A little persuasion had resulted in his speaking without further delay. When in Jaoa Tete, the English captain had been with Tshubaka Kambale, who was known to work for those who dealt in smuggled uncut diamonds from the Democratic Republic of Congo . . .

'Good God!' Tait exclaimed, for once expressing emotion. 'The motive *was* theft! Captain Sewell was carrying a load of diamonds back here to hand over to the men running this end of the racket and he was murdered by whoever nicked them out of the safe.'

'It's a possibility. But since no diamonds are known to have been in the safe, it can only be an assumption he was acting as a courier.'

'It would explain something that's been bothering us – why were only five dollars nicked?'

'That now ceases to bother you?'

'Until the diamonds were sold, they had no value for the thief and he knew it could take a long time to sell them, so he wanted something – call it a token – to provide himself with proof of success.'

After a moment, Campbell said: 'An imaginative explanation.'

'Criminals often have convoluted minds.'

'So one needs a convoluted mind to understand them?'

Bloody funny, Tait thought. Campbell possessed a sarcastic sense of superiority under that apparently good-humoured, bumptious manner.

'We can say one thing is for certain. Diamond smuggling wouldn't have been organized in the one trip; no one's going to meet a visiting captain for the first time and hand over a fortune. Sewell would have been approached and checked out. So he would have had to visit Porto Cavado before. Do we know if he did?'

'I can't say.'

'Find out. Whether in the *Hakota* or one of the other boats.'

Tait made his way to his present office – more a cubby hole. On his desk was the current file of the Sewell case and in it was the number of the telephone installed on the *Hakota*. His call was answered by the chief steward. Captain Sewell had been in command of the *Hakota* for the past six years and during that time she had visited Porto Cavado four times.

Tait reported to Campbell.

'It's possible you're right.'

I'm bloody sure I am, he thought.

'We're going to have to carry out a search. Not that we can expect much joy. The crew have been free to go ashore from the day the boat docked, so nothing would have been easier than to hand the diamonds over or post them.'

The search, carried out by ten uniformed police and two detectives, uncovered, to the bitter annoyance of the crew, fifty-one cartons of cigarettes, twenty bottles of whisky, eleven of gin, and fifteen kilos of hash (hidden in the funnel, to the astonishment of those who had thought the funnel of a ship was like a chimney), but no diamonds.

Thirteen

Tait looked through the window of the car at the bungalow, one of ten set around a large circular cul-de-sac. If the captain had been making an illicit fortune, he had not spent it on his home. The car in front of the garage was a Ford Fiesta, the number plate showing it was several years old.

He walked up to the wrought-iron gate, which showed signs of rust, opened that and entered the garden. The small lawn had the quality of a bowling green and the two shaped flower beds were filled with colour. Someone was a far keener gardener than he. The front door needed repainting. He rang the bell.

The door was opened to the length of a security chain. 'Yes?' said a woman.

'Inspector Tait, county CID. My identity card.' He held the opened card so that she could read it through the gap between door and jamb.

'One moment.'

The door was shut, there was the muted sound of metal against metal, the door opened and he faced an elderly woman whose severely featured and lined face reminded him of an aunt he had, with youthful maliciousness, called Virago Intacta. 'I rang you earlier, Mrs Sewell . . .'

'Come in.'

He entered a hall, lightly furnished with a small table on which was a bowl of roses, two framed etchings of modern steamers, and a mahogany coat stand. He shut the door.

'I'm very sorry about what happened, Mrs Sewell.'

'Thank you,' she replied formally.

'As I said over the phone, I should like to ask you some questions.'

'I don't understand why.'

'It is possible you may be able to help in the investigation into the unfortunate death of your husband.'

She seemed about to speak, but did not. She led the way into the sitting room, crossed to the television set and switched that off. 'Please sit.'

He settled on a well-worn chair and a wayward spring in the seat pressed uncomfortably into his right buttock, forcing him to wriggle to try to escape it. The television set was black and white, there was a threadbare patch in the carpet and two tiles in the surround of the fireplace were cracked and missing small pieces.

'Would you like some coffee?' she asked.

'Thank you, but I had some just before I left.'

'Then you can tell me what it is you want to know.'

Perhaps, he thought, the solitary life she had had to lead most of her married life had forced her to be so self-reliant, she appeared cold natured. Or perhaps that was the kind of person she was. Had the captain needed extra money to keep a young bit of skirt happy? 'We are doing all we possibly can to identify the criminal who so brutally attacked your husband, Mrs Sewell, but I have to confess that for the moment we are not meeting with as much success as we wish. One of our problems is that we cannot determine the criminal's motive. Every member of the crew speaks of your late husband with respect, yet obviously someone is lying. When he was last home, did he mention any unusual occurrence which happened the previous voyage?'

'I'm not certain I understand.'

'We think it possible Captain Sewell may have had reason to discipline severely one of the crew and this resulted in the man threatening him – something he might have mentioned to you.'

'He very seldom talked about his ship.'

She had spoken bitterly. Perhaps she had learned or suspected her husband had enjoyed the favours of more than one young lady; after all, tradition held that a sailor had a girl in every port.

'You see . . .' She began.

He waited.

'It doesn't matter.'

'Anything you can tell us might prove to be of considerable significance.'

She stared at the far wall with unfocused gaze as she said: 'When, because of his age, Patrick was compulsorily retired from the company with which he'd been all his working life, he wanted nothing more than to be at home so we could enjoy each other's company for the time we had left. But that couldn't be because of Basil. Patrick had to find another job to supplement his pension and the only company which would employ him at his age was Akitoa. I went aboard before he sailed with them for the first time and when I remembered the ships he had been commanding, I was so upset . . . That's why he never talked about what happened aboard.'

'Who is Basil?' he asked quietly.

'Our son.' She indicated a framed photograph on the mantelpiece.

He was close enough to see clearly the thin, slender boy in shirt and shorts, holding a rugger ball in his hands.

'He was at prep school.' Her tone became distant. 'He hated my taking the photograph because he said the other boys would claim he was becoming swollen headed. Boys are so cruel. But he had scored the winning try. And we'd just learned he was suffering the very early symptoms of primary lateral sclerosis and would not play much more rugger . . . Often when I see him, we talk about that game.

Originally, I didn't because I thought it might be too hurtful a memory, but he manages to gain pleasure, not bitterness, from the past. He's very brave.'

'He lives here with you?'

She shook her head. 'He did until I could no longer physically help him as he must be helped . . . The day I drove him to Bransbury was as mentally painful as the day the specialist told me what the prognosis had to be.' She turned her head away.

And now her husband was dead because some bastard had smashed in his head. Life loved to kick a person who was already on the floor. He stood. 'Thank you very much, Mrs Sewell. I know how painful it has been to talk about what happened.' A lie. He did not know how painful it could become to talk about the past and, pray God, never would.

He entered his room – broom cupboard – at divisional HQ and sat behind a desk which had probably been recovered from a junk yard. He opened the bottom drawer and brought out a local telephone directory. Bransbury Nursing Home was in large print. He dialled, spoke to a woman who asked him to hold. Moments later, a man said: 'Thornton speaking.'

'Inspector Tait, local CID. I'd be grateful for some information.'

'Such as, Inspector?'

'What are your fees?'

'That depends on the nature of the client's illness and the attention he or she will require. If you like to tell me—'

'What are Basil Sewell's fees?'

'He is a patient here?'

Tait checked what he'd been about to answer – sarcasm did not assist co-operation. 'That's right. And has been for some time, I understand.'

'Hang on.'

Receiver to his ear, Tait stared at the opposite wall on which hung a calendar from three years before.

'Are you there?'

No. He'd gone for a drink. 'Yes.'

'Basil's fees have just had to be raised to one thousand nine hundred pounds a month.'

'Good God!'

'I know it is a very considerable sum of money, but I can assure you we provide the best possible care and that has, unfortunately, become more and more expensive. Staff salaries, equipment, building regulations . . .'

'How long has he been in the nursing home?'

'I can't give you the exact figure unless I check past records and that will take rather a long time.'

'An estimate will do.'

'Perhaps five years.'

He thanked the other, rang off. Small wonder Sewell had sought extra income.

'What have you learned?' Campbell asked.

Tait, standing in front of the desk, was certain the books in the bookcase had been moved again. 'In my opinion, sir, we can accept that Sewell did not act as a courier of stolen diamonds – assuming he did – to make money for his own pleasures. His home is very ordinary and in need of considerable maintenance, it's poorly furnished, his wife dresses simply and wears no jewellery other than a couple of rings on her marriage finger. Their son is an invalid who's been in a nursing home for several years and the fees are now nearly twenty-three thousand a year. It's obvious he needed a further source of income if he was to keep his son there.'

Campbell tapped the desk with his fingers. 'That explains his dishonesty, but doesn't help us identify his murderer.'

'As to that, Mrs Sewell had nothing to offer After joining the Akitoa Company, he very seldom spoke about his ship. Obviously, he bitterly resented having to work in a tramp company and when at home, wanted to be a world away from it.'

'We're getting nowhere fast.'

'It happens.'

'Not when I'm running the case.'

Then you're a bloody miracle worker, Tait thought. Cases were always having to be pushed on to the back burner because the law, formulated by liberals untouched by consequences, often dealt the trumps to the criminals.

'I want officers and crew questioned again.'

'We're falling back badly on our regular work, sir, because of the large use of manpower in this case and the budget is becoming badly stretched . . .'

'I want everyone questioned again,' Campbell repeated with aggressive force.

Because you're frightened by what failure will do to your promotion chances, Tait said silently.

On Thursday afternoon, Marr entered the superintendent's office and waited patiently as the other spoke at length, and in strong terms, to the detective inspector of another division. Someone had made a balls-up, Marr judged happily. Other people's misfortunes afforded him satisfaction.

Campbell slammed down the receiver.

'I'm reporting that the questioning of the crew has been completed, sir.'

'And?'

'Nothing fresh, I'm afraid.'

'Then the wrong questions were asked.'

Marr stared at nothing in particular.

'Tell Inspector Tait I want a word.'

As he reached for the door handle, there was a further order. 'Forget that and tell Constable Ryan to come and see me.'

He went out and closed the door. The case was as good as in the dead file if a woman's help was needed.

Helen was not in the CID general room. Yates was.

'Where is she?' Marr asked.

'Who? The cat's mother?'

'Cut out the humour.'

'It's humour which keeps the world sane, sarge.'

'And sends useless detectives back on to the beat.'

'She was called out to a hit-and-run in Campton Frith; an old girl on her bike knocked down and injured.'

'When she gets back, tell her the super wants her.'

'Who doesn't?'

'You've a sewer of a mind.'

'Sewers are necessary.'

'Unlike you.'

Marr left. These days, the young were feckless, contemptuous of authority, and pursued pleasure before duty. He wished he was young again.

Fourteen

Helen entered Campbell's room as the last of the four strokes from the nearby church bell sounded through the half opened window. 'You wanted to see me, sir?'

'I'd like a word, yes.' Campbell stood, began to pace the floor, came to a stop. 'There's no charge for sitting.'

She settled on the chair to the side of the desk. He resumed pacing and she began to feel uneasy. When a senior officer appeared to be uncertain, trouble was not far away.

'This case is stalled. You'd not disagree?'

'We're certainly not making much progress at the moment, sir.'

'Who did you speak to when the crew were questioned for the second time?'

'Grainger, Jones, Calvert, and Grose.'

'Grose.' He crossed to his chair and sat. 'Still alibiing Tucker?'

'Very much so.'

'Do you believe him?'

'I'd put it the other way round. I could find no reason to disbelieve him.'

'Maybe you didn't try hard enough. Tucker has to be one of the strongest suspects.'

'When he has a solid alibi?'

'Grose may be lying.'

'When the case is murder? Why would he take the risk?'

'Bribery.'

'What can Tucker bribe him with?'

'A share in the proceeds of the diamonds.'

'Surely that's using an assumption, not fact, on which to base motive and execution?'

'You've a lot to say for yourself!'

'I like to say what I think, sir.'

'Have you considered the possibility of a homosexual relationship between Grose and Tucker?'

'I haven't, no.'

'Then you should have done since they share a cabin. That would provide a very strong reason for Grose lying.'

'Grose is not gay.'

'You're an expert on identifying a man's preferences?'

'Women are better judges than men. When Grose looked at me, he was undressing me.'

'You are an expert on thoughts as well as inclinations?' He stood, resumed pacing. 'This case is in danger of dying. I don't intend that to happen. Inspector Tait had a word with Mrs Sewell to find out if she could help us. She couldn't. He did, however, learn her only son has for some years been suffering from an incurable, progressive disease and is in a nursing home. Can you imagine her emotions when, on top of that tragedy, her husband is murdered?'

'Only with great difficulty.'

'When one meets such distress, one wants to do something, anything, to help. One might think there is no way in which one could, but experience has shown that isn't quite true. Someone who has suffered a crime often gains a measure of relief from knowing the criminal has been caught. I imagine it is the satisfaction of learning life can balance the scales of justice. That is why I am determined to crack this case, whatever it takes.' He paused, then said: 'You have a frank tongue, so answer this. If things continue as they are, will we identify the murderer?'

'It looks less and less likely.'

'Yet we've pursued all orthodox lines of enquiry. So what

does that tell us? That only an unorthodox line has any chance of being successful.'

He came to a stop and stared at Helen. 'You mentioned Dunn offered you coffee and cakes on the ship. So he was friendly, happy with your company?'

'I gathered he learned his wife had left him from a letter he received during the voyage; I guess he'll be happy with any company.'

'But not sufficiently happy with yours to suggest seeing more of you?'

'I don't see what that has to do with—'

'Bear with me and answer the question.'

'In fact, he did ask me to go out with him.'

'You accepted?'

'No.'

'Why not?'

'It hardly seemed right for me to become friendly with someone involved in a murder case.'

'In normal circumstances, how would you have reacted to his offer?'

'I'd probably have said I'd like to.'

'Then you will not be averse to seeing him socially?'

'But as I've just said—'

'Let me finish. I want you to make it clear to him that you would, after all, welcome further social contact.'

'Are you suggesting—'

'For God's sake, woman, I am not suggesting a roll in the hay. Just further contact outside the official inquiry which will give you the chance to learn if he can answer a few questions.'

'You want me to spy on him?'

'Have you ever been on observation duties?'

'Yes, of course.'

'That was spying.'

'There was every reason to believe the person under observation could help the investigation.'

'Well?'

'You're saying you believe Dunn could be guilty?'

'It has to be a strong possibility.'

'A moment ago, despite an alibi, you held Tucker was still a prime suspect. Now, you're virtually saying you don't think that.'

'Do you never keep your tongue in check?'

Rank could always win an argument.

'You seem, Ryan, to have forgotten we still don't know, though we suspect, why Dunn left a first-class company for a third-rate one.'

'Is that likely to be of real consequence?'

'Possibly. Probably. You questioned Dunn in the course of the investigation, which means he'll have been careful what he said, as is every witness, guilty or innocent; when Joe Citizen sees a copper approach, he remembers he's parked on a solid line. Speak to Dunn in relaxed circumstances and he'll not be on his guard because his mind will be occupied in wondering how soon he can make a move.'

'You said you weren't asking me to offer a roll in the hay.'

'You don't have to make any offer for him to wonder.'

'I don't like it. Using a salacious interest to entrap him.'

'Captain Sewell didn't like being murdered. Mrs Sewell doesn't like being a widow.'

'I'd rather not go ahead.'

'Taken a shine to him?'

'I judge him to be a decent man who doesn't deserve to be emotionally betrayed in the name of justice.'

He pushed back his chair and paced once more. 'Do you know Donne?'

'Only very vaguely.'

'"Any man's death diminishes me, because I am involved in mankind." When someone's murdered, I not only feel diminished, I feel bloody angry because the murderer has not only destroyed his victim, he's ruined the lives of all those who knew the victim . . . Remember what I said earlier?'

'With reference to what in particular?'

'The only relief we can offer Mrs Sewell is to arrest the bastard who killed her husband.'

'The result always justifies the means?'

He stopped pacing and sat on the edge of the desk. 'I visited her in order personally to assure her we are doing everything possible to identify her husband's murderer; also to say that her husband's personal belongings which were on the ship are safely in our hands and will be given to her the moment they can be released. The young so often think the old can bear pain and sorrow better than they, but of course that's nonsense. I have never before seen such stark misery as she was suffering. I'll be perfectly frank, I wanted to run away and escape. If you'll agree to what I'm suggesting, there's the chance of learning something which will lead to a breakthrough and so enable us to bring her some mental relief; continue to refuse and there can be no such chance.'

He spoke with such force, she felt that for Mrs Sewell's sake, she was morally obliged to do as he asked. It was only after she had left the office and her own emotions had calmed, that she remembered Tait had visited Mrs Sewell and so it seemed unlikely Campbell would also have done so.

Fifteen

As Dunn stepped out of the booby-trap of number two hold, he saw Helen walk from a car towards the ship. He made his way aft and reached the gangway as she stepped down on to the deck.

She smiled. 'I'll bet when you saw me, you said, My God! Not that woman again.'

'I told myself it's my lucky day after all.'

'I'm feeling generous, so I'll believe you.'

'Stretch your generosity to having coffee and cakes with me.'

'When I've specifically come earlier than before so it wouldn't seem as if I wanted to abuse your hospitality yet again?'

'You'd abuse it by refusing. I'm told the baker has excelled himself today and the cakes are pure ambrosia.'

'You're testing my will-power to breaking point.'

'The greatest enjoyment is to let it snap.'

As they made their way up to the smoke-room, he was certain their frivolous conversation meant she was as glad to see him as he was to see her.

Calvert was in the third officer's cabin, making the bunk.

'Bring some coffee and cakes along to the smoke-room, please,' Dunn said from the doorway.

'I don't reckon Butchy will have made them yet.'

'Test how correct your reckoning is by asking him.'

'I've got to finish this cabin and then do the fourth's.'

'Since the fourth is ashore at company's office, any delay won't inconvenience him.'

Calvert plumped the pillows with unnecessary force. 'I suppose it's for two?'

'Your supposition is correct.'

'In your cabin?'

'I said, the smoke-room.'

'Don't remember you saying that.'

'There's none so deaf as choose not to hear.'

Dunn returned to the smoke-room and sat. 'There may be a slight wait if the cakes aren't quite ready.'

'I seem to remember your saying they were and were pure ambrosia.'

'You force me to admit that that was a minor terminological inexactitude.'

'Call it deceitful – it's shorter.'

'It is often said that a wish to deceive can be a sign of flattery . . . What brings you back?'

'The superintendent wants one or two things checked.'

'Such as?'

'Whether the cakes are just as delicious.'

'That is aggravated deceit since you said you'd arrived early to avoid the suggestion you were here for sustenance . . . All right, I'm being curious and asking questions I shouldn't.'

Their conversation became casually inconsequential until Calvert entered the smoke-room with a tray. He put this down on the table, left.

'He doesn't look a happy man,' she said.

'Few stewards do . . . Will you be mother?'

She pulled the tray closer to herself. 'How do you like your coffee? Black or white?'

'In port, white, at sea, black.'

'Why the difference?' she asked, as she picked up the coffee pot and poured.

'A couple of days after sailing, we're reduced to powdered

milk whose only resemblance to the genuine article is that it's white. It makes coffee taste of old socks.'

She passed him cup and saucer. 'Do you like being at sea?'

'The job resembles the curate's egg; in parts good, in parts, bad.'

'Which predominates where you're concerned?'

'Largely depends on the skipper. He makes for a happy ship.'

'What decided you to go to sea?'

'A boyhood belief it was romantic and foreign ports were exciting.'

'You sound thoroughly disillusioned.'

'Nothing as impersonal as the sea can be romantic and see one port, you've seen them all.'

'Why didn't you go into the Royal Navy if you wanted glamour and excitement?'

'My father advised me very firmly I'd never become amenable to mindless discipline and so my career would be short and inglorious. He was probably right.'

'What for you constitutes mindless discipline?'

'An order made solely for the sake of giving an order; demanding something be done which needn't, or even shouldn't, be.'

'And that happens only in the Royal Navy?'

'Far more often than in the Merchant Navy.'

'Give me an example.'

'I sailed with a chief who was an apprentice during the war on a ship which was torpedoed in the South Atlantic; the skipper managed to sail her into the Azores, where she was patched up with concrete, but it left him doolally and from then on, he insisted when in port all the bridge brightwork was polished – binnacles, speaking tubes, telegraphs, port rims – knowing full well that as soon as they set sail, all this would have to be gunged up to avoid reflecting sunlight and alerting a sub.'

'That's a long time ago.'

'Things seldom change. Skippers still bolster their egos by giving stupid orders.'

'Did Captain Sewell?'

Dunn stirred his coffee. 'I've always thought of him as possessing two opposing characters – a good seaman and a nit-picking skipper.'

'You both admired and despised him?'

'I suppose so.'

'When you take command, will you eschew the slightest suspicion of mindless discipline?'

'I hope so.'

'You doubt your ability to do that?'

'Command can change a man.'

'In what way?'

'At sea, a captain is monarch, prime minister, lord chief justice, and commissioner of the Metropolitan police force. It can be difficult to keep one's balance when that omnipotent.'

'I'm sure you'll manage to.'

He gained pleasure from her words.

She brushed cake crumbs from her fingers on to the plate, looked up at the electric clock on the bulkhead. 'I'd better start work or the sergeant will accuse me of spending my time drinking coffee and eating delicious cakes.'

'Is there anything I can do?'

'I don't think so, thanks.'

'How long will it take?'

'I've no idea. Why do you ask?'

'I thought you might like a drink before you return ashore.'

She smiled. 'How did you guess?'

He was by number two hold when Yates came for'd and spoke to him. 'A young lady is asking if you've caught the train to London?'

He looked at his watch. 'Damn! I didn't realize how long I've been.'

'I offered to keep her entertained, but she politely declined.'

'She's no fool.'

'Despite that, you're making progress?'

'Between us, we're rewriting the Kama Sutra.'

Yates briefly wondered if perhaps Dunn was not joking. 'By the way, Brian's turned up in the smoke-room and is trying his luck.'

Dunn made his way aft, pausing briefly at number three to check the square of the lower 'tween; it was not clear of cargo, but in less than an hour it would be and then the hatch boards and beams would be lifted and the unloading of the lower hold would begin – if the stevedores failed to think up an excuse to strike.

The third officer was talking earnestly to Helen. Dunn was glad to note she looked less than enthralled. 'Sorry to have been so long, but I ran into a problem.'

'Without serious injury to the softer parts, I hope?' Moran laughed loudly. 'I'm offering drinks in my cabin, chief.'

'Very generous, but you need to go aft and stay a while to make certain the new runner has been rigged at number six and—'

'I've had a word with the bosun and it's all fast.'

'You can still make certain things are running smoothly.'

'But—'

'As sharp as you like.'

Moran left, his annoyance obvious.

'I wonder,' she said, 'if contrary to your declared intentions, that was an unnecessary order.'

'It was very necessary since two's company, three's an argument . . . How about that drink?'

'I've realized it's a little early . . .'

'Not when the sun has risen well above the yardarm.'

'Has it? Tell me, what is a yardarm?'

'Either end of a ship's yard.'
'This is going to take time. What is a yard?'
'A beam on a square-rigger supporting a sail.'
'It goes up and down a mast?'
'That's one way of describing it.'
'And the bottom yard will be low down?'
'Yes.'
'So the sun rises above it fairly early in the morning?'
'Unless one's in the Arctic or Antarctic.'
'Small wonder it's such a popular gauge of when to start drinking.'

They went along the cross-alley and into his cabin; she sat on the settee.

'As before, I'm afraid the choice is restricted to gin, whisky, or lager.'

'I enjoyed the pink gin you gave me, so I'll choose that. But, please, more water than before.'

He poured the drinks, handed her a glass, sat. 'Happy days. And many of them.'

She drank, lowered the glass. 'It's not everyone who enjoys many, is it?'

'Probably not.'

'Remember saying to me we were both in the same boat?'

'Of course.'

'I never realized how leaky my boat was until it was sinking.' She drank. 'At first, everything was sunny. Dean and I had fun and talked about life when we were married. Then I returned home sooner than expected to find him packing. When I asked him what was up, he hummed and hawed before admitting he'd met a woman who'd blown his mind, amongst other things. Tried to tell me he'd always remember me with gratitude; I made it very clear I'd remember him as a coward who'd been trying to sneak off while I was at work because he hadn't the guts to face me . . . Was it anything like that for you?'

'In some ways.'

'You'd rather not talk about it?'

That was true, but he felt under an obligation to do so because she had been frank about her affair. 'We'd had arguments. Who doesn't? They were mostly over money. When aren't they? I tried to make her understand we had to economize, that credit had to be repaid on time, but she wouldn't listen. Things weren't too serious whilst I was in the Beltrane Line, but when I joined this outfit, she lost all sense of proportion and I had to take out a second mortgage on the house. Yet she still went on spending and the last time I was home, I was shocked to find out how much we owed. After reading her letter in Porto Cavado, telling me she was off, I've wondered if spending more than we had was a way of showing resentment. She was always socially ashamed of my being in the Merchant Navy and not a stockbroker or merchant banker, but the Beltrane Line had a good enough name to keep her resentment in check; when I moved to Akitoa, there was no such restraint.'

'Do you know the man she's gone to?'

'A good friend. Or was.'

'That's extra cruel. What was the attraction?'

'A sixteenth-century moated manor house which provided a home fit for a gentlelady.'

After a moment, she said: 'How different from hope life usually turns out to be.'

'Hope is the opium of the people.'

'What a sad thought . . . For heaven's sake, why are we depressing ourselves like this?'

'The human desire for disaster.'

'You're talking nonsense.'

'Give me time and I'll recite brillig and slithy toves.'

'You're not half the pessimist you make yourself out to be, are you? Confess that's true.'

'There are moments when I'm lightly touched by optimism. So I'll ask, are you still as busy as you were a week ago?'

'How do you mean?'

'You can't remember?'

'Modesty demands I don't.'

'I wouldn't have thought you over modest.'

'Is that complimentary or critical?'

'Are you still too busy to have dinner with me?'

'Tonight, I'm afraid the answer has to be, yes.'

'And tomorrow?'

'I'm not doing anything for several days.'

'We have a date?'

'I hope so.'

'This calls for another drink.'

'The sun has climbed another yardarm?'

Helen had just greeted Yates and sat down behind her desk in the CID general room when Marr looked in. 'So it was you!'

'Doing what?'

He stepped inside. 'You've finally honoured us with your presence! Where the hell have you been?'

'Enjoying coffee, cakes, and a couple of drinks on the *Hakota*.'

'You reckon you're paid to enjoy yourself?'

'If I did, I'd complain about value for money.'

'I've a mind to have you up before the inspector.'

'If I were you, I'd have second thoughts.'

'You don't sodding well tell me what to do. Just because you've got two tits—'

'Sarge, I was obeying orders.'

'Pull the other one.'

'Too painful. The superintendent ordered me to go on to the ship and talk to Dunn in a friendly manner.'

'Like horizontally,' Yates suggested.

'Didn't you know vertical was now the fashion among the haut monde? It prevents clothes creasing.'

Marr said with impatient anger: 'He told you to go aboard and amuse yourself?'

'Check with him if you don't believe me.'

'As if we didn't have enough to do without wasting time because of your goddamn stupid ideas.' He stepped out and slammed the door shut.

'Were you genuine?' Yates asked.

'You think I'd risk lying when he can so easily check me out?'

'But wouldn't because that would be like criticizing the super's orders and Campbell would chew his necessities into pulp . . . So what's the game?'

'The super reckons Tucker is the prime suspect, despite the alibi, but Dunn runs him close. So he wants to know Dunn's history and in particular why he left the Beltrane Line.'

'And?'

'And I'm to chat him up to find out what I can.'

'With legs crossed or uncrossed?'

'To prevent your imagination going into overdrive, I am not offering a roll in the hay.'

'Hay gets into all the wrong places.'

'Personal experience?'

'My scene is black sheets. Would you like me to show you mine?'

'If you must. But there's no way I'm going to show you mine.'

Sixteen

Helen was about to go down to the canteen for a light lunch when she was told the superintendent wanted to speak to her. She went along to the detective inspector's room.

'I've been expecting a report,' was Campbell's greeting.

'I tried to find you when I returned from the *Hakota*, sir.'

'Next time, try harder . . . Well, what's there to say?'

'Dunn's wife was very extravagant and the debts were sufficient for him to have to take out a second mortgage. It's my guess that the house is at risk of being repossessed.'

Campbell leaned back in his chair. 'Now we're beginning to see some light. He needed money and needed it fast . . . Why did he change companies?'

'I haven't learned that yet. I didn't want to seem too curious in case he started wondering why.'

'You've fixed to see him again?'

'Tomorrow evening.'

'Why didn't you make it this evening?'

'I'm seeing an ancient aunt.'

'Couldn't you have put her off?'

'I could, but wasn't going to. The poor old girl sees hardly anyone and looks forward to my visits.'

Campbell expressed his annoyance at her faulty priorities. 'Find out why he changed companies. Take your time, but hurry it.'

'Something of a contradictory order, sir.'

'An insolent comment.'

'Do you mind if I say something?'

'Like as not, you'll say it anyway.'

'I think you're making a mistake regarding Dunn as a serious suspect.'

He stood and paced the floor, came to a stop by her chair. 'Have you never learned it's undiplomatic for a constable to tell a superintendent he's making a fool of himself?'

'I have not said that, sir.'

'You've suggested it, right enough . . . Why is it a mistake to suspect Dunn?'

'He's not a thief or a murderer.'

'Proof of that?'

'It's difficult to prove a negative. I'm going by instinct.'

'Hardly a relevant way of judging innocence or guilt.'

'The more I see of him, the more certain I am that he's innocent.'

He resumed pacing. 'The captain was on the bridge because of the fog and there was every reason to believe he would remain there until the fog cleared. But he was taken short and returned downstairs to his room, to find a man stealing a packet of uncut diamonds from his safe. That man thought if he was to escape a charge of theft – not accepting the captain could hardly admit to the loss of smuggled diamonds – he had to kill the captain . . .'

'Sir.'

'What?'

'Dunn was on the bridge and knew the captain had gone below. He didn't leave the bridge during his watch.'

'The only evidence of that is his own.'

'How would he have known where the keys of the safe were? Tucker had every chance of finding out because he was in and out of the cabin, probably often when the captain was on the bridge. Dunn would only have occasionally gone there and that when the captain was present.'

'Won't you allow him as much practical common sense as you showed when you suggested they might be in the desk?'

'But that's because I had the experience . . .'

'The guilty man had to have the opportunity to enter the cabin unseen. Dunn had that. He had to have reason to steal. Dunn was in considerable, perhaps overwhelming debt. Dunn had a further motive for murder – the captain's assessment of his abilities which might well prevent his gaining command.'

'We've never checked if Tucker has form. He could legitimately enter the cabin at any time. He had to kill if he was to retain the diamonds.'

'And he has a solid alibi.' Campbell crossed to his chair and sat. 'Have you made the mistake of exceeding your assignment?'

'I don't understand the question.'

'Have you mixed business with pleasure?'

'You're suggesting what?'

'That you're becoming too involved to make solid judgments.'

'Then you'd better take me off the case.'

'And you'll cease seeing him?'

She hesitated.

'Carry on. But remember, I want facts, not emotions.'

That was great coming from him, she thought. How had he inveigled her into spying on Dunn?

The restaurant was not typical – the staff were pleasant and efficient, the food lived up to the menu descriptions, and the wine was not excessively overpriced. They sat at a corner table, close to a large, framed photograph of a range of snow-covered mountains in sharp sunshine.

The wine waiter asked if they would like liqueurs; Dunn looked at Helen and she shook her head. He refused.

She drank the last of the coffee in the small cup. 'I have

enjoyed this,' she said, as she replaced the cup on the saucer.

'Then we'll do it again.'

'On one condition. We go Dutch.'

'We'll see.'

'You'll find I'm a woman of my word.' She experienced momentary self-denigration because she had become a woman of lies. 'How did you learn about this place?'

'A friend who prefers quality to fashion recommended it some time ago, but this is my first time here.'

'Do you live close to Coalpool?'

'Just outside the village of Stetchford.'

'Isn't that where there's a rather gorgeous manor house with very elaborate wrought-iron gates?'

'The place seems to hold a fascination for women. It's where my wife is now living.'

'Oh, God! I'm sorry.' She reached across the table and briefly put her hand on his. 'Forgive?'

'How were you to know?'

'I've always wanted to live in the country.' She spoke quickly, to leave her gaffe behind.

'But you haven't?'

'I was born and lived for years in London suburbia. Then the firm for which I was working was relocated to Coalpool and I moved down. A year later I finally had had enough of sitting in front of a computer and joined the police. When Dean and I became a twosome, I suggested we found somewhere in the countryside, but as he said he didn't want to die from boredom, we ended up in town. Still, unlike London, ten minutes in a car takes me out to green fields, woods, space . . . Do you live in an old house with oak beams, peg tiles, a ghost?'

'A clapboard cottage which is less than a hundred years old and is ghostless, but not devoid of memories. It's surrounded by a one-acre field and when the wind's from the east, there's the delicate scent of pigs. My neighbour's an enlightened farmer who detests modern factory farming and lets his herd of Gloucester Old Spots roam around an ancient orchard.'

'It sounds great.'

'It was.'

She looked quickly at him, then away. 'I suppose we'd better move. I'm on early turn tomorrow.'

'What does that mean?'

'On duty from six to two in the afternoon.'

'A pity. I was going to suggest, subject to your not minding the driving, a run in the countryside even if it will be nearly dark.'

'Dusk can be the prettiest time of the day, so on second thoughts, I'll believe Trevor or Gavin will cover for me.' And on third thoughts, her conscience insisted on adding, however late she reported for duty, she could cite Campbell's orders as a valid excuse. 'Let's go to the Devil's Dyke. At night, there's a patchwork of lights and darkness which reminds me of an illustration in a book I enjoyed immensely when I was young.'

She parked the car facing south on the enlarged shoulder of the road which provided a viewing point. The dyke was a forty-yard-wide, grassed gash in the sharply sloping land. The sea was still just distinguishable by the line between it and the sky.

'What was the book?' he asked.

'How's that?'

'What was the book with the illustration?'

'Sorry, I was miles away.'

'Where?'

'In the land of wishes.'

'What were you wishing?'

'Like her age, a lady's wishes are at her discretion . . . I can't remember the name of the book, or the author, but there was this illustration of the prince setting out with his retinue, all of whom carried flaming brands. I thought him terribly brave because the forest was filled with dragons and he was going to rescue the princess. He succeeded, of course, after all sorts of terrible dangers.'

'And they lived happily ever after?'

'I expect so. In my day, children's books were still allowed to be romantic. It's a pity romance has disappeared . . . You know the story of this dyke, of course?'

'No.'

'The devil was roaming the countryside when he came across an old abbot whom he reckoned would be an easy victim. But the abbot ran so quickly, it took the devil a long time to catch up with him and then, just as the devil was about to grab hold of him, he produced a crucifix. The devil had to press both hooves into the ground to prevent himself crashing into the crucifix and he did so with such force, he gouged out this dyke and that slowed him down and the abbot was able to escape. The devil was so enraged that every fourteen years he comes up from hell and grabs hold of any man he finds and carries him off. Unfortunately, no one knows when the fourteen years begin and end.'

'Then we could be at risk?'

'You could, but not me.'

'Which is why you were prepared to come here to enjoy the view?'

'I felt certain you were a quick runner.'

She stopped at the open gateway and the dock policeman came out of the small hut.

Dunn lowered his window. '*Hakota.*'

The policeman waved them on.

They rounded the cargo shed and came to a halt by the gangway.

'Happiness should be pursued with racing feet or it will escape,' he said. 'Since you offered me the choice of nights, you must be free tomorrow?'

'Dutch.'

'We'll see.'

'You won't, if you don't agree right now.'

'I'm forced to succumb to your blackmail.'

'I'll pick you up here instead of in town – that'll save you having to catch a bus.'

'What time?'

'Six, because I'll need to freshen up.'

'Spend a little less time in front of the mirror making-up and settle for five thirty.'

'I use very little make-up.'

'So I've noticed with approbation.'

'You don't prefer green eyeshadow, rouged cheeks, and Day-Glo lipstick?'

'On you? Why improve perfection?'

'In the face of such hyperbole, I'm speechless. Five thirty, then, unless my sergeant creates problems.'

'Smile and you'll have him eating out of your hand.'

He climbed out of the car, went round the bonnet, to say goodbye. Her window was half down and her face was illuminated by the light from the arc lamp on the foremast of the *Hakota*. He would have kissed her had he not suffered the impression she hoped he would not.

As he boarded, he wondered if his impression had been nonsense; or, if correct, why had she hoped he would not.

'I had dinner with him,' Helen said.

'And then?' Campbell asked.

'We went for a drive to the Devil's Dyke . . .'

'I'm not interested if you went all the way to Shangri-La. Did you find out why he changed shipping companies.'

'No, sir.'

'Why not?'

'I didn't want to rush things.'

'Unlike him.'

'If you're interested, he behaved like a gentleman.'

'You had to fight him off in the first five minutes?'

The male mind never matured. 'I'm seeing him again tonight.'

'Then get your mind fixed on what you're meant to be doing.'

'I'd rather forget that.'

'I've a piece of advice for you. Curb the desire to say what you think. It's not every senior officer who'll put up with an insolent detective constable, even if she is female.'

'I hope I'm never insolent, sir.'

'Hope is a bloody poor substitute for fact.'

When he said nothing more, she left.

Seventeen

Lewis, seated on the settee in the smoke-room, put his cup down. 'You wouldn't like to do my watch for me, would you, chief?'

'You're quite right,' Dunn answered.

'It's Sunday.'

'So I believe.'

'With no cargo being worked, there's no call on us.'

'Then your duty should not be onerous.'

Lewis helped himself to the last cake. 'How long have we been stuck here?'

'This is the twelfth day,' Moran said. 'Twelve days when we ought to be at home, enjoying life. If we'd any gumption, we'd tell Captain Barton he can shout as much as he likes, we're off.'

'So lead the way.'

Moran muttered something.

'I phoned Rosie last night.' Lewis bit off a piece of cake, spoke through a mouthful. 'She says she's getting bigger by the hour.'

'When is it due?' Dunn asked.

'Another six weeks according to the hospital, but I can't believe they're right. She can't keep growing all that time . . . Been on at me again, wants me to quit the sea and find a shore job. It gets rough for the wives when we're at sea and they're on their own.'

'Except for when the milkman calls,' Moran said.

'What's that supposed to mean?'

'Nothing.'

You can't believe a wife can be faithful, can you?'

'All I was saying—'

Dunn interrupted him. 'If you spoke a lot less, life would be more pleasant for others.'

'Christ! Anyone would think this was a seminary.'

'An unlikely mistake when you're present.'

'I'm clearing off before you lot start singing hymns.' He left.

Lewis fidgeted with the handle of his empty cup. 'Rosie has been very upset recently, what with one thing and another. One of the old girls on the estate has been alarming her with tales of what can go wrong. Two-headed babies, that sort of thing.'

'Tell your wife not to listen to a load of balls.'

'I did. Hasn't stopped her worrying . . . You don't have kids, do you?'

'No.' Estelle had insisted she wanted to enjoy life rather than suffer motherhood.

'Sick every morning. The doctor says that's quite normal. I suppose all suffering is normal to a doctor.'

'But very unwelcome to the rest of us.' Dunn stood.

'I was hoping to get home to cheer her up a little. I could be back aboard inside a couple of hours.'

'If I hadn't a date which can't be altered, I'd stand in for you.'

'Oh well, I'll just give her a phone later on . . . She'll probably go on and on about me swallowing the anchor. I'd like to, but I'm not qualified for anything else. I mean, what's a mate's ticket good for ashore?'

A question many a seaman had asked himself without finding an answer, Dunn thought as he left the smoke-room and made his way along to his cabin. He changed into civvies, checked the time and found he had twenty minutes in hand. As eager as a teenager, he thought sarcastically.

Helen drove up to the gangway at five thirty.

'Dead on time,' he said, after greeting her. He sat, pulled the passenger door shut. 'A woman of her word!'

'That surprises you?'

'No.' But it did confirm one difference between her and Estelle.

She backed and turned the car, drove around the cargo shed and up to the gates. The dock policeman looked out through the opened doorway of the hut, offered them a brief wave.

'I wondered if you were interested in birds?' she asked, as she accelerated. 'The flying kind, perhaps I should add. We've time before we eat, so I thought you might enjoy a visit to the bird sanctuary.'

'That would be interesting.'

'You sound doubtful.' She braked to a halt at lights.

'Only because I can hardly tell a blackbird from a crow.'

'Perhaps you need glasses . . . There are usually a number of species, especially duck.'

'You're a keen ornithologist?'

'By accident.'

'That sounds intriguing.'

The lights changed and as the car in front pulled away, she accelerated. 'When Dean cleared out with the redhead, I felt . . . You'll know how I felt. Anyway, there were times when I wanted to get away from everyone and everything and I started to visit the sanctuary because there, there was space and usually solitude. It annoyed me to look at birds and not know what they were, so I started learning something about them. It became quite exciting to see a rare incomer . . . To other matters. Do you like Italian food?'

'Very much.'

'Then we'll eat in a small restaurant which opened last year. The proprietor is Greek, but he reckoned Greek food wouldn't be as popular as Italian, so he changed his name and nationality.'

'Trattoria Ronchi?'

'You know it?'

'It's where Estelle and I had a meal together before I sailed this last trip.'

'Then I've made the worst possible choice and I'll quickly think of somewhere else.'

'There's no call for that. It's ridiculous to let the past upset the present.'

'Sometimes it's impossible to stop it.'

'Right now, the past for me is out of sight.'

'I'm glad of that,' she said softy.

They left the restaurant and walked to the council car park. She settled behind the wheel of the Fiesta and inserted the key, but did not start the engine. 'The night's still young and I'm wondering if you'd like to come home and have some coffee and a liqueur to aid digestion . . . That is, provided you like Tia Maria, which is all I have?'

'It would make a perfect end to a perfect evening.'

'There's just one thing.'

'Which is?'

'The invitation is for coffee and a liqueur only.'

'I wouldn't imagine otherwise.'

'You're one of the few men I know who's maybe honest when he says that.'

'Yet you felt the need to issue the warning?'

'Feminine insurance.' She drove down to the barrier – open because fees were not collected after eight at night – and out on to the road.

Twenty minutes later, she opened the front door of the third-floor flat and led the way inside. 'Go in there and I'll be with you when I've made the coffee.'

He went into a rectangular room, furnished lightly. The small bookcase contained mainly paperbacks and, convinced one's choice of reading to a degree reflected one's character, he read the titles. The westerns had to be Dean's. On the mantelpiece above the blocked-up fireplace was a photograph of Helen with a man who had a full beard. He had always regarded with suspicion men with beards. He sat.

She entered, a tray in her hands; he stood, took the tray from her, set it on a low octagonal, glass-topped table. She poured out two cups of coffee. 'I'll get the Tia Maria. Do you like cream on the top?'

'Painting the lily!'

'Risk the indulgence.'

He laughed. 'Not much of a risk.' He watched her leave the room, then added milk and a spoonful of sugar to one of the cups of coffee.

She returned, handed him one glass, sat. 'I hope you enjoyed the meal as much as I did, in spite of memories?'

'I told you, the past is out of sight,' he said forcefully.

'Good . . . Tell me, Felix, are you intending to stay at sea?'

'It's a job I like. And as the second said just before I came ashore, of what use is a ticket when it comes to looking for a job ashore?'

'What's a ticket?'

'A certificate to say one has passed exams and is competent to hold the rank named.'

'Which one do you hold?'

'Extra master's.'

'Which, presumably, is the top? So what are you qualified to command? *Queen Mary Two*?'

'Qualified, but not in the running.'

'Why not?'

'One, because I'm not in that line; two, because . . .' He stopped.

'Well?'

'An officer from a tramp company is as welcome in a crack passenger company as would be a hang glider pilot in the cockpit of Concorde.'

'Concorde's retired and the hang glider pilot probably

doesn't have an extra master's ticket . . . You're obviously ambitious, I've been told you're really good at your job whatever the captain said, so why don't you aim higher than the Akitoa Shipping Company?'

He finished his coffee, picked up the glass. 'There have been problems.'

'There usually are.'

'Most especially for bloody fools.'

'You're saying you're one of them?'

'An extra master one.'

'Nonsense. Your feet are far too firmly on the ground.'

'Does it matter?'

She assured herself that what she was doing was not because Campbell had ordered it, but because she was convinced Dunn could not be guilty of theft and murder and what he told her might help prove his innocence, not his guilt. 'Not if you'd rather not talk about it. But frankly, I just can't understand you being content to work in a third-rate company when you ought to be in a first-rate one.'

After a moment, he said: 'I was. The Beltrane Line.'

'You didn't like it?'

'It didn't like me.'

'More fool it.'

'They only had my word.'

'Your word for what?'

'For what really happened.'

'Were—' she began.

'Let's forget it.'

'But you can't forget it, can you?'

After a moment, he said: 'No.'

'And it hurts.'

'Of course it bloody well does . . . Sorry.'

'For what?'

'Being crudely rude.'

'Why shouldn't you be crude and rude if life's kicked you hard?' She drained her glass, put it down, stood, crossed to his chair and rested her hands on his shoulders. 'You've obviously been through one hell even before your wife left you; I went through mine when Dean cleared off. When one's suffered, one has to seek out one's own compensation. We've both earned the right to do that.'

'We may have earned the right, but life's indifferent as to whether or not we ever find it.'

'So it's all up to us.'

He stared up at her, said nothing.

'Felix, my love, it's the prerogative of a woman to change her mind. So now I'm offering a little more than coffee and a liqueur.'

It was sufficiently warm for them to lie naked on the bed, her head resting on his shoulder, her left arm across his chest. The curtains were drawn, but enough street light came through to form a pattern on the ceiling. He stared at this as he decided he had to answer her questions, asked and unasked, if their relationship was to be an honest one. He spoke in a low, even voice, as he allowed memories to surface.

SS *Calliope* had been a container ship on her third voyage. The accommodation, if compared to the *Hakota*, had been luxurious. Cabins were large, well furnished, and air-conditioned. In the smoke room had been a well-stocked library, television, a DVD player, and a film projector with a screen lowered from the deckhead. Satellite technology allowed those aboard to speak to their families at home. On the bridge, GPS enabled the deck officers to know exactly where they were at the press of a button with an accuracy no sextant could match . . .

Edward Kemp had claimed descent from Kempville de Tray, who had arrived in England with William the First. If true, Kempville had probably made certain he played no active role in the conquest. Kemp was smart, intelligent, lazy, and so full of his own importance that he resented even the mildest criticism. In Melbourne, where he had spent overmuch time with a girlfriend who lived in Cotham Road, Dunn's criticism of him for slackness had been so sharp, he had sworn he'd get even.

In Southampton, the five thousand cases of ten-year-old Islay malt whisky had been loaded in the strongroom, despite the fact that each case had to be carried there by hand because it was below the accommodation; whisky of whatever quality was every docker's prime target. The first officer was responsible for all cargo stored there – he locked and sealed the only door when loading was complete, he unsealed and unlocked the door when discharge was about to begin. He kept keys, seals, and sealer in his possession at all times.

The day before the discharge of the whisky in Sydney was to begin, Kemp had entered Dunn's cabin and said the captain wanted him up top, p.d.q. He'd hurried up to the bridge – no one there; after a while, he had gone down to the captain's flat – the captain was not there either. He'd waited, but after a further quarter of an hour, he'd shrugged his shoulders and returned below.

On the Thursday, he'd broken the seals on the strongroom door, unlocked it, and discharge had begun. The cases were tallied out of the strongroom, tallied on to the quay, tallied into the security area in the cargo shed. The three tallies had agreed – two cases of whisky were missing. The police were called.

The thief had broken the seals, unlocked the door, stolen the whisky, resealed and relocked the door. In the circumstances, Dunn became suspect. He became the prime suspect when a bottle of Laphroaig was found wrapped in an old sweater in the bottom of his cupboard. His protestations that he had never seen the bottle before had provoked sarcastic amusement – perhaps it had been teleported from the strongroom. Why didn't he admit his guilt and save everyone a lot of time and trouble?

Faced with the desperate need to prove his innocence, he had recalled Kemp's telling him the captain wanted to speak to him and that he'd been away from his cabin (which, carelessly, he'd left unlocked, but then it had never occurred to him a fellow officer might commit theft) long enough for Kemp to collect seals, sealer, and keys, break into the strongroom, take two cases of whisky, replace everything in his cabin and plant a bottle of whisky in the cupboard in the hopes it would be found by authority, thus getting his own back for the verbal blasting he had previously suffered.

Much as Dunn disliked accusing anyone, it had been necessary for his own sake to tell the police about the way in which Kemp had inveigled him away from his cabin. They had spoken to the captain and were informed that indeed he had demanded the presence of the chief officer, but had suddenly been called ashore. As the police had then pointed out, the main prop of Dunn's accusation – and his defence – had been knocked flat. They'd added sarcastically it was not unknown for a guilty person to place the blame on someone else in order to try to shift it from himself . . .

In the end, the police had reluctantly decided not to prosecute him. There was no direct evidence, apart from the bottle in his cupboard, that he had been involved in the theft; they could not prove the negative, that someone had not gone into his cabin and left it there; and the strongest point in his favour was that he had been able to prove, through the evidence of others, he disliked and never drank whisky. If he disliked it, why steal it? To sell? Then why keep one bottle? To offer it to others when to do so would immediately expose his guilt? . . .

The Beltrane Line had not been concerned about the niceties of legal proof. He'd been in charge of seals, sealer, and keys, so either he had been negligent in guarding them – which he had, leaving the cabin unlocked – or the Sydney police were far too generous. A senior director had offered him the choice of resigning or being sacked.

He'd consulted a solicitor about bringing proceedings for wrongful dismissal. The solicitor, pleasantly, made it clear Dunn was being naive, probably because he was a seaman. Proof required in a criminal case had to be stronger than in a civil case. If he brought an action, the court might well consider the evidence against him as being sufficient to declare he had no grounds for succeeding, and it was explicitly stated in his contract of employment that theft would incur instant dismissal. Also to be considered was that, whether or not he was successful, the details of the case would be in the public domain and inevitably the media would publish them since sea, whisky, and theft by an officer would provide a story for the public, who always welcomed the pillorying of someone in authority.

'So you didn't bring an action?' she asked.

'Had I done and lost, as the solicitor seemed certain I would, I'd have been publicly branded a thief and that would have damned any chance of my getting another job, even in a company like Akitoa.'

'Did you ever face Kemp?'

'He denied everything. Said someone else had seized the opportunity of my cabin being unlocked when I was up top. And . . .'

'And?'

'He sounded genuine.'

'You believed him?'

'I had to have someone I could blame.'

There was a long silence. 'Would Kemp have placed that bottle in your cupboard if he knew you didn't like whisky?'

'A detective's question? You're wondering if most of what I've told you is wishful imagination.'

'That's a filthy thing to suggest.' She moved until her head was above his. 'I know you were totally innocent because you've told me you were.'

'The way you put the question . . .'

'Habit, for God's sake, habit. If a case becomes confused, asking a question at the centre of the problem may start simplifying everything.' She kissed him. 'We've both been through black times, but we've both found colour again. Don't let's lose that.' She moved her hand down his body.

Eighteen

Helen sat at her desk in the CID general room and stared into space. What was she going to say to Campbell? How flexible a mind was there beneath that arrogant, domineering manner? Would he appreciate a man could, because of the person he was, be telling the truth however much circumstances suggested he was a liar?

'Enjoying memories of last night?' Yates asked.

She jerked her mind back to the present. 'How's that?'

'Are you reliving every exciting moment, every pulsating second, of last night?'

'I had a drink, supper, watched the television, went to bed.'

'May one ask, with whom?'

'Only if you've a mind which can't climb out of the dirt.'

'"The lady doth protest too much, methinks."'

'Think what you damn well like.' She knew she should have answered his questions with the usual facetious vulgarity since that would have stilled his curiosity, but conscience paralysed the mind. She stood.

'In a hurry to return to nirvana?'

'No.'

'Satiated for the moment?'

She crossed to the door.

'Experimentation is the way to renew appetite.'

She left and made her way to the inspector's office.

'Well?' Campbell demanded.

'I had a meal with Dunn last night.'

'Successfully?'

How was she to answer?

'Come on, woman, did you learn anything?'

'Yes, sir.'

'Then would it be too much trouble to tell me what that was?'

'He had an unfortunate experience when he was with the Beltrane Line.'

'What the hell does that mean? He was raped by a female passenger?'

'Another officer was a liar and a thief and ready to see an innocent man convicted for his crime.'

'Are you going to tell me what you learned in simple English or do I have to sit here and wonder if you're speaking Farsi?'

'Dunn was chief officer on one of Beltrane Line's most modern container ships. They loaded cases of Islay whisky in Southampton.'

'Which brand?'

'Laphroaig.'

'Liquid gold . . . Well, is that the full story?'

'The cases were tallied into the strongroom. Dunn had full responsibility for the safety of everything stored there and when loading was completed, he sealed and locked the only door. The seals, sealer, and key were always kept in his cabin. When the whisky was tallied out in Sydney, two cases were missing.'

'You mean, stolen?'

'Naturally, Dunn was questioned. At first reluctant to do so, finally he had to tell the police that the third officer, Kemp, whom he'd had reason to criticize very severely, had made certain he was away from his cabin by saying the captain wanted him. He'd gone upstairs, but the captain wasn't in his room, so he'd waited for quite a time – long enough for Kemp to pick up seals, sealer and keys, nick two cases from the strongroom, relock and reseal, return everything to Dunn's cabin, where he left one bottle in the cupboard, almost certainly not as a gift but in the hopes that if it was decided there had been theft and not mistaken tallying, it would be found by authority.

'The police spoke to the captain, who said, yes, he had called for the chief officer but had suddenly had to go ashore. This made Dunn's accusation look stupid and put him even more firmly under suspicion, but eventually they decided there was insufficient evidence to charge him.'

'Even though a stolen bottle was found in his cupboard?'

'They couldn't prove it had not been put there by someone else.'

'Didn't know the Aussie coppers kept their noses so close to the rule books.'

'Another thing, Dunn was able to prove he never drank whisky. When the ship returned home, Dunn was told he could either resign or be sacked. He wanted to take the company to court, but was advised by a solicitor it would not be in his interests to do so. He resigned and later joined the present outfit.'

Campbell suddenly thumped the desk with his fist, making her start. 'I knew that change of shipping companies was the key to the case.'

'Dunn did not steal the whisky.'

'And the moon is made of cheese.'

'I'm certain it wasn't him.'

He stood, paced the floor. 'Once a thief, always a thief. He was short of money because his wife spent like crazy. He'd discovered the captain was carrying diamonds back to England and decided here was the chance to solve his past, present, and future financial problems. Get into the captain's quarters, prove his hunch was right and the key was somewhere obvious, unlock the safe, nick the diamonds, and leave. A foolproof scheme because the captain wouldn't dare shout he'd been blagged.

'Intention and opportunity came together when the ship

ran into thick fog. The captain was on the bridge and wouldn't leave it until the fog cleared. Dunn, out on the wing, could leave unseen by both the captain and the man at the wheel. What he hadn't allowed for was the captain being taken short. So the captain found him in the middle of the blagging and he had to smack the captain on the head with something nice and solid – later chucked over the side – and arrange the body to make it look as if the captain had fallen on to the edge of the table.'

'I'm certain it didn't happen like that,' Helen said. 'Dunn did not kill the captain.'

'He had motive, opportunity, and form. What more do you need? A written confession?'

'You've said more than once that Tucker has to be the prime suspect. He was in and out of the captain's cabin every day, so he had the perfect opportunity to learn where the key of the safe was kept. He knew the captain would be on the bridge all the time there was fog . . .'

'You've forgotten he has a solid alibi?'

'It must have been bought.'

'You know that for fact?'

'Grose is providing it because he's been paid to.'

'Assumptions don't go down well in court.'

'Haven't you been making a whole raft of assumptions about Dunn?'

Campbell came to a halt and stared at Helen for several seconds, went round his desk and sat. 'I'm wondering if you've become very friendly with Dunn despite your previous pious reservations.'

'Meaning?'

'If you don't understand, I'm not going to spell it out.'

'Because I might lay a complaint against you of sexual harassment?'

'Get out.'

She left.

Nineteen

Helen was barely aware that what she was eating was shepherd's pie and runner beans.

'You're very far away,' Wiseman said, as he sat opposite her at one of the six tables in the canteen. 'Problems?'

'Kind of.'

'Something we men don't have to put up with, thank God!'

She was grateful he should make the mistake; it satisfied his curiosity.

'Is there anything I can do which would give you the chance to slide off and take things easily for a while?'

'Thanks, Trev, but it'll take my mind off problems if I keep working.'

'Just give me a bell if you need help.'

'I will.' Wiseman was the kind of man she labelled huggable.

A couple of moments later, he said: 'Have you heard about poor old George?'

'What's happened to him?'

'He was chasing a suspect, fell, and broke his arm; means he'll miss the final of the ballroom competition.'

'I'd no idea he was into that scene.'

'He does look more like a scrum forward, doesn't he, but I've heard he's real smart when it comes to whirling around the dance floor with his wife. Of course, she's tiny and as light as a thistle. Shamus reckons she always has to be on top or she'll suffer peine forte et dure.'

'That's the kind of thing he would say.'

'He can be amusing.'

'Depends on one's sense of humour.'

'I'll be moving.' He stood, collected up plate, knife, fork, saucer and cup, walked away.

She'd provided poor company. But she could not stop imagining what the consequences might be of what had happened.

Dunn was talking to the bosun by No 6 boat, when Campbell, followed by Horne, climbed the port ladder to the boat deck and walked across.

'I'm damned if I'd want to spend time in that.' Campbell indicated the lifeboat.

'You won't find anyone keen on doing so,' Dunn said dryly.

'What's it say? Thirty-six persons. Worse than the Black Hole of Calcutta . . . Have you time for a chat?'

'I can make time.'

The bosun, his very broad shoulders out of proportion with his body, walked aft.

'We'll go along to the captain's flat,' Dunn said.

He led the way into the short cross-alley and the day room. He sat on the chair by the desk, leaving them the two easy chairs which were secured to the deck.

'We'd be grateful if you'd answer one or two questions,' Campbell said, as he settled. 'Is it correct your wife has left you?'

'I don't see that that is any concern of yours.'

'I'm afraid we have to be concerned with many things, Mr Dunn. Would you describe her as an extravagant person?'

'What the hell is this?'

'An extravagant person who spent like crazy, leaving you debts so serious you've had to take out a second mortgage on your house to meet them?'

'Who gave you authority to investigate my private affairs?'

'I need to remind you this is a murder case?'

'No.'

'Then surely you are happy to give us all the assistance you can?'

'Give it, not have it taken.'

Campbell briefly smiled. 'You will agree that when your wife left you, you found yourself in considerable debt? Debt which had the potential of leaving you unable to maintain repayment of the mortgages?'

'I have a job – or has that escaped your burrowings into my private affairs?'

'When a man faces the loss of his home, he's likely to panic. Did you panic? Did you say to yourself, you had to keep your house, no matter at what cost?'

'What exactly are you getting at?'

'Am I correct in believing the Beltrane Line pays its officers more generously than Akitoa does?'

'Yes.'

'Then were you still employed by them, you would be in a better financial position. Why did you leave it?'

'Personal reasons.'

'Because the company believed you had stolen two cases of whisky in Sydney?'

Dunn knew sharp mental shock.

'They gave you the option of resigning or being sacked. That's so, isn't it?'

'I did not steal the whisky.'

'The company was convinced you did.'

'The police said I was innocent.'

'The Australian police decided there was insufficient evidence to charge you, which is a very different matter. As we have the misfortune to know, all too often we are certain a man is guilty, yet are unable to charge him because the courts will not accept there is sufficient hard evidence.'

'Someone else stole the whisky.'

'As you told the police, giving them chapter and verse. Only when they checked, they found chapter was wrong and the verse was balls.'

'There was one good reason why I didn't steal it.'

'Because you never drink whisky?'

'Who told you all this?' Dunn demanded hoarsely, knowing the answer.

Campbell ignored the question. 'When did you first learn the captain of the *Hakota* was running uncut diamonds?'

'When I was told that after we got back here.'

'It must have seemed the answer to your prayers. Steal the diamonds and the captain couldn't complain because what he was doing was highly illegal. You wouldn't know how to go about selling them, but reckoned you'd very soon learn. So in one smart move, you could save your house, wipe out all your debts, and afford a snappy little number to keep your bed warm.'

'That's nonsense.'

'Ideas are easy, carrying them out can be tricky. How to open the captain's safe without his knowing? The fog provided the answer. He wasn't expected to leave the bridge all the time the fog was thick and that gave you an easy run. Only your luck ran out because he was taken short and found you helping yourself. Which meant you had to kill him.'

'That's crazy.'

'Why not tell us where the diamonds are and maybe earn yourself a brownie point for helping the law?'

'I've never seen them.'

'Why are you talking so soft? Because you're smart and realize the one place where there would be no search or only a cursory one was this room, since this is where the diamonds were stolen. Or two, they are in your own room where, in a ship you know backwards, they're unlikely to be discovered. Or three, you've sent them to your home.

So to find out which possibility is correct, we're going to carry out a more thorough search aboard and, if necessary, of your house.'

'You've no right to do that.'

'I have obtained a search warrant.'

'You'll find nothing.'

'You'll discover that our expertise in searching is greater than yours in hiding.'

'Think yourself as clever as you like, you won't find any diamonds because I didn't steal them and I didn't kill the captain.'

Campbell spoke to Horne. 'There's some take half a lifetime to learn.'

'And some who never do learn,' Horne replied.

'If . . .' Dunn began, then stopped.

'Well?'

'If I didn't kill the captain, someone else did.'

'Your logic can hardly be faulted.'

'I saw someone going along the boat-deck not long before the captain left the bridge.'

Campbell spoke to Horne. 'Do you remember Mr Dunn previously making a statement to that effect?'

'No, sir.'

'And nor do I. Interesting!'

'I didn't mention it because . . . I thought I recognized him, but couldn't be certain because of the fog.'

'And you were reluctant to put a possibly innocent man into the frame?'

'Of course I was.'

'Because you remembered how your accusations concerning Kemp had rebounded on you?'

'Because I couldn't be certain.'

'Who was this man you're so reluctant to name?'

'Tucker.'

'You recognized him?'

'I thought I did.'

'Then I have to tell you, you were mistaken. Tucker has an alibi which says it's impossible he was on the deck at around six that morning.'

'Then it was someone who looked like him.'

'Who would you suggest?'

'How can I suggest anyone?'

'Names seem to come to you easily enough.'

'When I'm telling the truth, not surmising.'

'A truth which becomes flexible when it's advantageous to blame someone else. We'll start our search as soon as Constable Horne has called the others along to help us.'

Horne left the cabin. Campbell folded his arms across his chest and stared into space. Dunn silently tried to deny to himself he had told only one person about Kemp and the stolen whisky.

Horne turned into the gravel yard which fronted Rosehip Cottage and braked to a stop. Campbell stepped out of the car, waited until Dunn was standing near him, said: 'A perfect situation if you own the land around the house. Do you?'

'Yes,' Dunn replied.

A second car arrived and three uniformed constables got out of it. Campbell ignored them. 'Late nineteenth century?'

'Early twentieth.'

'Does the boarding have to be repainted often?'

'It should be done every three years.' For Dunn, reality was moving ever further away. They were here seeking the proof he was a murderer and thief, yet Campbell expressed interest in the house . . .

Campbell spoke to Dunn again. 'Will you lead the way?'

Dunn crossed the yard and opened the gate – which Estelle had demanded he paint on his next leave because it looked so shabby, it embarrassed her when friends came. He went around the corner of the house and along the brick path, unlocked the door, momentarily hesitated. He had wondered what it would be like to return to an empty house. Now, a suspected murderer and thief, he was learning.

'We'll start upstairs,' Campbell said, when everyone was in the hall. 'I'd like you to be with us all the way, Mr Dunn, to prevent any suggestion of planting evidence. Not, of course, that I believe you would ever do such a thing.'

Sneering was a childish trait, his mother had said when he'd scornfully mentioned one of the boys in his form was stupid enough to think bacon came from cows.

He went up the stairs. He'd made the brightly coloured, patternless carpet at sea, to the amusement of the second. Estelle had never liked it. It was not fashionable to have homemade carpets.

In the attic, they used small metal tools, like old-fashioned toast forks, to search through the insulation pellets and an underwater torch to make certain there was nothing in the cold water or central-heating overflow tanks. In the bedrooms, cupboards were opened, drawers emptied, mattresses turned over and checked for cut stitching, carpets lifted; in the bathroom, cupboard and low-level cistern were examined; in the kitchen, the refrigerator offered only a half-full bottle of milk which had gone rotten and was hastily emptied; in the larder, every tin or jar was carefully examined to check if it had been opened and then resealed; in the dining room, one of the constables lay on the floor and, with the aid of a torch, made certain there was nothing taped underneath the sideboard; in the sitting room, chairs and cushions were prodded and checked for signs of interference, the carpet was lifted, every book was taken from the small bookcase and opened up, the back was removed from the television set; in the sewing room – as Estelle had called it although she had seldom sewed anything – a loose floorboard was carefully lifted . . .

They gathered in the hall.

'You've found s.f.a.,' Dunn said.

Campbell was unable to hide his frustrated annoyance.

'Which proves I had nothing to do with the theft of the diamonds.'

'It says you were sufficiently far-sighted to foresee the search. I congratulate you on your choice of a hiding place.'

'Have you finished?'

'Yes.'

'Then you can clear off.'

'You don't want to be taken back to your boat?'

'No.'

They left.

Dunn went into the larder, the top shelf of which was the bar. On this were bottles of gin and whisky, a third and a half full, three bottles of tonic, four cans of lager, a bottle of bitters, and some white vermouth which was growing whiskers. He poured himself a pink gin, went into the sitting room, and sat. He tried to convince himself he must have drunk too much during a pre-lunch session aboard and have talked too freely about the reason for his leaving the Beltrane Line. But hard as he tried to believe in that possibility, he couldn't. Drunk out of his mind, he would not have told other officers the truth because that was too painful and humiliating to be mentioned except to someone one loved and whom one wanted to understand . . .

The phone in the hall rang.

A cold-call, trying to sell him something? Had Estelle seen or learned about the car's arrival at the cottage? The ringing continued. A cold-caller would have given up, Estelle would only persevere if she wanted something and living in the lap of luxury, what could she lack? He put his glass down on the piecrust table, went out into the hall and across to the corner cupboard, lifted the receiver. 'Yes?'

'Felix?'

He recognized Helen's voice, said nothing.

'Can you hear me?'

'Yes.'

'Aren't you on your own?'

'I am now.'

'I've just learned the superintendent, Gavin, and three uniforms have been in your place. What happened?'

'They found nothing. Which will surprise you.'

'Of course it doesn't. I knew they wouldn't.'

'Really? When you'd fed them enough information to make me suspect numbers one, two, and three?'

'No!'

'You didn't tell them about Kemp and the missing whisky; that the Australian police suspected me of having stolen it?'

'My love, please listen—'

'You wanted to know why I changed companies, but reckoned I wouldn't tell you voluntarily, so you invited me to your flat to make things easy.'

'You . . . you're suggesting I went to bed with you to persuade you to tell me? In God's name, how could you think that?'

'Easily.'

'Can't you understand?'

'You don't understand that I understand perfectly.'

'I'd never have let you touch me if I hadn't loved you.'

'You sound as if for the moment you're finding it difficult to live with yourself.'

'You don't believe I'm in love with you?'

'Betraying me proves something, but I wouldn't call it love.'

'The superintendent became convinced the reason for your leaving the Beltrane Line would help prove you were guilty of the murder of Captain Sewell and the theft of the diamonds. I was hoping it would help prove your innocence . . .'

'Hoping so hard that when we were in bed, you doubted what I'd told you.'

'I didn't.'

'You couldn't understand why Kemp planted the bottle of whisky on me.'

'I explained that.'

'And I believed you. Which makes me wonder how I could have been so naive.'

'I swear all I wanted to do was help.'

'I hear you.'

'Felix, it was my duty to report to the superintendent . . .'

'Then I trust you explained how thoroughly you exploited all your assets to compile your report.'

'I tried to make him understand it couldn't have been you . . .'

'Rather a difficult task after you'd told him about the *Calliope*.'

'He's searched everywhere and found nothing, so he'll have to start accepting your innocence.'

'Is that why, just before he left, he complimented me on being sufficiently far-sighted to find a good hiding place?'

'He was bloody-minded because he'd been proved wrong. Searching your house has helped you.'

'You have an interesting way of looking at things.'

'Why won't you understand?'

'As I said, the problem is, I do.' He replaced the receiver.

He went along the hall, to the larder and poured himself a second and stronger pink gin.

Twenty

The first of July reminded people that summer's lease had all too short a date. The cold easterly wind provided a suitable partner for the grey sky and drizzle.

Tait and Marr sat at the table in the conference room and waited, their conversation brief. Campbell hurried in, slid on something and cursed as he grabbed hold of the table for support, went round to the end chair and sat. 'I've had the ACC on the blower,' he said bitterly. 'County has had Akitoa Shipping on its back. The company lawyers are demanding the crew be released to go on leave or a fresh crew will have to be found when the ship sails. That makes too much commercial sense for us to refuse their demand unless we can show we're poised to wrap up the case. Can we claim that?'

No one answered immediately, then Tait said: 'We're working on several leads.'

'Which are up blind alleys.'

'We know Dunn was chucked out of his previous company for theft—'

'Which isn't proof he nicked the diamonds and murdered the captain.'

'But it's an indication.'

'We tell the lawyers we know who's guilty, but can't prove it just yet, so will they hang on for a few weeks? . . . I'm going to have to tell the ACC we can't claim to be close to an arrest. You know what he's going to say to me?' Campbell spoke with growing anger. 'He'll ask what in the bloody hell have we been doing the past fifteen days – farting in the wind?' He pushed the chair back, stood, began to pace. 'I want Grose questioned again.'

'You reckon Tucker is still in the frame, in spite of Dunn . . .' Tait began.

Campbell came to a stop, leaned forward and rested his hands on the table. 'We failed to find the diamonds when we searched the captain's quarters and Dunn's house, but that doesn't prove his innocence; it only proves he's cleverer than we are at the moment. So we have to get cleverer than him. In the meantime, I want Grose questioned because we have to appear to be doing something and aren't as clueless as we are.'

All show, Tait thought. Confirmation that Campbell had only made superintendent through influence, not ability.

Grose entered the smoke-room, came to a halt and stared at the far bulkhead. 'You wanted me?'

'Grab a seat.'

Grose's eyes were close together, he blinked repeatedly, and he did not happily stare straight at another person; his lips were too thin, his cheeks too full; not a man to whom one would cheerfully lend a fiver, Tait thought as Grose sat.

'We've a few more questions,' Tait said pleasantly. 'But first there's something I want you to understand. Listen carefully and say if there's anything which bothers you.'

Grose took a pack of cigarettes from his pocket. 'D'you mind if I light up?'

'Suit yourself.'

'Will you have one?'

'I don't.'

'And you?' Grose held out the pack to Yates.

'Thanks all the same.'

He put the pack on the table, brought out a cigarette, lit it.

Tait spoke smoothly. 'It's perfectly normal for one person to want to help another, but there can occasionally be times when it is the wrong thing to do. You follow me?'

'Yeah.'

Tait opened the file on the table and read for a moment, looked up. 'You know a person can be charged and convicted of the offence called an attempt to pervert the course of justice?'

'I'm afraid I don't know what that's all about.' Grose spoke with obsequious deference.

'It means deliberately doing or saying something in order to prevent the law arriving at the truth. So a man who lies to the police in order to help a friend escape the consequences of a crime, a very serious crime, can expect to be sentenced to many years in jail.' Tait turned to Yates. 'Do you think that makes it clear?'

'Crystal clear,' Yates answered.

'Mr Grose can be under no illusions about the seriousness of attempting to lie to us?'

'Not a chance.'

Tait once more looked down at the top paper in the folder. 'Grose, you've told the police what you know about the events of the morning of June the sixteenth – that's the day the captain was murdered. Do you remember being questioned?'

'Yes, and I helped the best I could only I didn't know nothing.'

'What I want to do now is see if you can add anything to what you told us before. Which reminds me, I should have explained something else. The law acknowledges there's a big practical difference between a mistake and a lie. If a man tells the police something and later realizes he's inadvertently made a mistake and explains this to the police, there can be no question of him being charged with perverting the course of justice . . . You shared a cabin with

Tucker, the captain's steward, during the voyage. How do you get on with him?'

'Not so bad.'

'You're friendly?'

'That's it.'

'Very friendly?'

'Like normal.'

Grose had given no indication that 'very friendly' held any special connotation for him. Helen had probably been correct when she had decried the possibility of the relationship between Grose and Tucker being a homosexual one. 'We'll talk about the morning the captain was killed. Do you know anything which would help us name the person who killed him?'

'Can't say I do. I mean, if I could, I'd of said before.'

'Where were you that morning at around six?'

'In me bunk.'

'Were you on your own in the cabin?'

'Arnie was there, in his bunk.'

'You're referring to Tucker?'

'Yeah.'

'He hadn't taken refreshments to the captain who'd been on the bridge all night?'

'The old man had said as when he wanted something, he'd send word. Arnie hadn't heard nothing.'

'So Tucker slept on?'

'He weren't asleep. We was chatting.'

'What about?'

'Football. He goes for Arsenal and me for Spurs and he was all cocky because we'd heard Arsenal had beaten Spurs. I said it was only because the ref gave a wrong penalty, but he said that didn't matter because Arsenal won by two goals, so I said you get a wrong penalty given against you and you're all upset.'

'You remember the conversation in some detail. Why's that?'

'How d'you mean?'

'I could not tell you what I talked about several weeks ago.'

'I suppose . . . Well, I suppose people remember when it's something really interesting.'

'When did Tucker leave the cabin?'

'Him and me went for breakfast.'

'At what time?'

'Eight.'

'And then the two of you did what?'

'Went back to the cabin and had a chat and a smoke.'

'A chat about what?'

There was a silence.

'You don't remember?'

'Have to think.'

'You had no difficulty in remembering when I asked you what Tucker and you talked about earlier.'

'That was easy.'

'Why?'

'It just was.'

'Routine makes it difficult to distinguish one day from another. So if you had said that you couldn't remember what you'd been talking about before breakfast, I'd not have disbelieved you. But when you can describe in detail one conversation and remember nothing about another held shortly afterwards, I think there's a reason for so inconsistent a memory. And when I wonder what that reason might be, I come up with the answer that the first conversation was rehearsed to make certain you and Tucker said the same thing, while you never thought to agree a second conversation so now you're afraid of saying something completely different from what he may have said or say.'

'It ain't like that.'

'Why would you have rehearsed that first conversation? To provide Tucker with an alibi. What has he promised you in return for your lie?'

'I don't understand what you're saying.'

'I'm trying to persuade you not to be a fool who spends several years in jail because you keep telling us the same, sad story. So we'll offer to forget what you've just been saying if you admit you've been worried ever since the police first questioned you because you made a mistake, but have been afraid to say so. At sea, day follows day and nothing but the weather changes. The morning you and Tucker had that chat about football might well not have been the morning the captain was killed; you just can't be sure, can you?'

There was a long silence.

'I know what day it was,' Grose said hoarsely. 'It was the day he died.'

Tait silently swore.

'You ballsed it up,' Campbell said.

Tait stared at the framed print – his print – which hung on the wall behind the desk – his desk.

'Didn't pressure him.'

'Couldn't bend the rules any harder, sir.'

'A cadet could have done better.'

'I questioned him exhaustively.'

'Questioned? More like a chat with cucumber sandwiches.'

'He's smarter than he looks.'

'I wish I could say the same for you.'

'I pointed out that if he continued to lie, he'd be charged with attempting to pervert the course of justice. I suggested he could get himself out of the problem by saying he accepted he could have made a mistake in the day . . .'

'Yet you came away with empty hands.'

'We'll work on him and he'll start to sweat.'

'When he's sailed off and is thousands of miles away?'

'Get the company to take him off the *Hakota* so he stays back here in the UK.'

'They'll jump at the chance to do us a favour after all the grief we've caused them, won't they? Especially when we can't justify the request with proof.'

'Then the case could be heading for the dead file.'

'It's already there, thanks to incompetence.'

Failure was going to mark both their careers, Tait thought bitterly.

As Dunn entered the captain's day room, Captain Barton said sharply: 'I've been sat here waiting half the bloody day.'

'The seaman couldn't find me, sir, because I was down number three, where there are several crushed crates.'

'Deliberately crushed?'

'I doubt the dockers are sufficiently interested in copra. Much more likely, inefficient dunnage.'

'Didn't you check the loading?'

'A complaint of lack of four-by-four for dunnage was made, but the shore office said there was no more available.'

'Make certain that's down in your report . . . I've heard from the police. They're closing down the investigation in a clear admission of failure. Failure that's cost the company a bloody fortune and is going to cost another because the whole crew will have to go on leave at the same time, which means I've got to find a skeleton dock crew.'

'When does leave start?'

'Tomorrow.'

'That's very short notice . . .'

'Don't give a damn what it is. Leave ends on the twenty-third.'

'There'll be more moans about the short time.'

'Can't be helped. Your relief will be here in the morning. I want your cargo report before then.'

'I'll see you have it, sir. Who'll be the skipper next voyage?'

'Not up to me. If it were, it would be you. Since head office will decide, it'll probably be a cabin boy.' Barton walked past Dunn, came to a brief halt in the doorway. 'Have a good leave.' He left.

What were the odds against his having a good leave? Dunn wondered.

Half an hour later, as he was finishing his report on the damaged cargo, an AB stepped into the day room. 'There's a call for you, sir, on the land line.'

'The marine super?'

'A lady.'

'She didn't give a name?'

'Couldn't quite catch it. Something like rain.'

Ryan. He knew fresh bitterness. The pain of Estelle's betrayal had been overwhelmed by his love for Helen. But she also had betrayed him. 'Say I'm ashore and you don't know when I'll be returning aboard.'

Twenty-One

Dunn dropped his two suitcases in the boot of the taxi – observing tradition, the driver had made no effort to help him – and settled in the back seat. 'Which dock?' the driver asked.

'Four.'

'Is that the old tramp?'

'The *Hakota*.'

'Sooner you than me, chum,' he said, as he drove across the station forecourt. 'Looks like it ought to have been scrapped years ago.'

Dunn stared through the window at the passing town. Coalpool's high street had been taken over by multiples and resembled every other main street in the country; only the old part of the town retained character.

The taxi drew up by the gangway of the *Hakota* and Dunn paid the driver, who left him to retrieve his suitcases. He boarded, went along to his cabin. Young, tall, thin, more cheerful than his elongated face suggested, was seated at the desk. Young stood, waited for Dunn to drop the two cases, shook hands.

'So they've got you relieving,' Dunn said.

'For a few weeks.'

'When did you leave the *Howea*?'

'One trip back. Went ashore for my master's.'

'Successfully, I hope.'

'I scraped through, despite my brain trying to scramble in the viva voce.'

'I know the feeling. So when do you put up the third gold band?'

'Inside the year, with any luck. Mike Adams is retiring and Bill Peters will likely get command, so there'll be a mate's job going.'

'This calls for a drink to celebrate.'

'No one's arguing! . . . You had a trip and a half, by all accounts!'

'It had its moments.' He moved past Young and opened the cupboard door, brought out a bottle of gin, one of bitters, and two glasses.

'I gather the police still don't know who did the old man in.'

'Not for lack of trying.'

'How's that?'

'They made everyone's life hell.'

'And the old man was smuggling uncut diamonds. There's a turn-up for the books. If you'd asked me, I'd have said the sour old bastard had never so much as pinched a Smartie when he was a kid. Just goes to show you never really know someone, you only think you do.'

Words to deepen his gloom. He passed a glass to Young, sat, drank.

'Your new skipper's aboard.'

'Who is he?'

'Langdon. D'you know him?'

'Only by reputation.'

'Which isn't far wrong by my calculation. He didn't realize I was relieving and asked me up to his cabin for a drink; said he liked to get to know his officers because that made for a happy ship.'

Small wonder Young had spoken sardonically, Dunn thought. An unwelcome quality in a captain was friendliness since it indicated a weak character – a reluctance to accept the resentment authority must incur. He drained his glass. 'I need another drink.'

* * *

Yates knocked on the door, stepped into Dunn's cabin. 'Morning, captain.'

'Acting captain no longer; the new skipper's aboard.'

'A bit like being assistant chief constable one day and PC the next, then?'

'Probably not quite so dramatic a demotion.'

'Still, there's many who reckon it's better to stay just under the top because then one can duck when the mud's flying . . . I'm here to say Inspector Tait's bringing Mrs Sewell aboard this afternoon at around four and would be very grateful if an officer can meet them.'

'Coming aboard for why?'

'She's collecting her husband's belongings.'

'She hasn't had them long before now?'

'She was asked to come and fetch them a time back, but wouldn't. So Inspector Tait got in touch again and said as you'd be sailing tomorrow, if she wanted the stuff, she'd have to move.'

'Why weren't they just parcelled up and sent to her?'

'It was thought better if she collected them so that if anything's missing, she can't finger us.'

'Surely she'd never think one of you would steal her dead husband's things?'

'Experience says people'll think anything.'

'Where is his gear?'

'It was in his room, in a box we sealed. If you'd like to make certain that's still there so there's no problem when she comes aboard to collect everything?'

'Will do.'

'And you'll be here this afternoon?'

'Barring accidents.'

'I'll be on my way, then. Good to see you again.' He left.

Had that been Yates's way of saying he had never believed he had murdered the captain? Dunn wondered sarcastically.

He made his way up to the captain's day room, knocked on the door.

'Come in.' The captain sat at his desk. Tucker was in the doorway of the bathroom.

Dunn was wearing civvies, so he identified himself. 'Chief Officer Dunn, sir. Just back from leave.'

'Glad to meet you, chief.' Langdon stood, came forward and shook hands. 'Judging from Captain Barton's comments, I'm lucky to have you aboard.'

Sewell would not have said that to an archangel. 'One of the detectives has just spoken to me and said Mrs Sewell is coming aboard this afternoon to collect Captain Sewell's gear. It's in a box that's been sealed by the police and I wondered if you knew where it is?'

'I don't, but I'm sure Tucker does.'

'In the starboard locker by your desk,' Tucker said.

'You're taking it now, chief?'

'I think it ought to stay where it is, sir, so the police can check it's as they left it. They obviously have to be very careful about that sort of thing.'

'Very well. By the bye, I'd like to have a word with Mrs Sewell to say how sorry I am about her husband's dreadful death.'

'She'll be aboard at around sixteen hundred hours.'

'I'll make a point of not going ashore until later.'

Dunn crossed to the door.

'Who does the cargo plan, chief?'

'The third, sir.'

'Would you be kind enough to tell him I'd like a word as soon as possible? I want to explain that I prefer a particular colour scheme to be used.'

Red, white, and blue? Dunn wondered, as he left.

He met them at the head of the gangway. Mrs Sewell, in black, was first and he offered her his arm for support, but she ignored it and stepped down on to the deck. Tragedy had not softened her. Her features remained glacial, her manner autocratic. 'Good afternoon, Mrs Sewell.'

She inclined her head.

'Is the captain here?' Tait asked, as he followed.

'In his quarters,' Dunn answered. Yates was looking enquiringly at him and he nodded – the box of Sewell's possessions was ready. He led the way up to the captain's flat.

Langford hurried to say how saddened and shocked he, and everyone else, was by the death of so great a man. 'I have arranged to have coffee . . .'

'Nothing for me,' she said. 'Where are they?'

'In that cupboard, Mrs Sewell,' Dunn said. He crossed to the starboard locker by the desk, opened it and brought out the oblong cardboard box which had been sealed with police tape. He put it down on the desk.

'We have an inventory of the contents,' Tait said, 'so if you'd be kind enough to check the items.'

She might not have heard.

He nodded to Yates, who stepped forward to the desk and tried to break the plastic tape with his hands; it was too strong and he had to use a penknife to cut through it. He opened the top flaps of the box, brought out a small object wrapped in newspaper, unwrapped an inscribed silver ashtray.

As she stared at this, her lips began to quiver. She held out her hand. When he gave the ashtray to her, she gripped it tightly and from the back of her throat came sounds which differed only slightly from those made by a woman enjoying an orgasm.

They were shocked and embarrassed by her violent distress. Dunn recalled with angry self-contempt his judgment that tragedy had not softened her.

During the next fifteen minutes, as the items were unwrapped and checked, each man wished himself somewhere, anywhere, but where he was.

The last item was a silver-framed photograph of her in a wedding dress in front of the door of a parish church – daffodils were in flower to her right.

She said shrilly: 'Who killed him?'

'We are still investigating—' Tait began.

'Why isn't someone locked up for the rest of his beastly life? How am I to live when I know the man who murdered him is alive and free? Oh, God, is this what you call justice?'

Stations had been called, but Dunn had not yet left his cabin and gone for'd. He stared through the square port of his cabin at the blue sky above the roof of the cargo shed. The knowledge that her husband's murderer was free was only less painful to Mrs Sewell than the knowledge of his death. Whether it was her desire for revenge or the certainty that only the conviction of the guilty man could begin to make sense of the murder to her, he could not judge. But what was certain was that she would find a measure of relief from the murderer's arrest. Helen must have known from her work that this would be so, which was why she had acted as she had. She swore she had sex because she loved him; he had felt the need to tell her about his past. She had faced two opposing duties – to keep silent for his sake or to pass on the information to the detective superintendent in the hope it might assist identification and conviction. She had chosen to honour the latter, while knowing the possible consequences of so doing. It had been the need to help an emotionally savaged woman, not treachery, which had motivated her. When he had accused her of treachery, he had been cruelly wrong.

He hurried down to the chief steward's cabin, asked for the phone.

'Sorry, chief; it was taken off an hour ago.'

He went out on deck and along to the gangway. The

lamptrimmer and two hands were preparing to hoist and stow. 'Hold it,' he ordered.

'The pilot's aboard, sir, and the bridge has said to hoist.'

'Just hold it.'

He raced down the gangway and along to the end of the cargo shed where there were two public telephones. One had been vandalized, the other was being used. He asked the speaker, a docker, if he'd hurry things up and was told to bugger off. Ten minutes later, the docker left.

He inserted money, dialled.

'Start Road police station.'

'I must speak to Detective Constable Ryan.'

Minutes later, the man said: 'Constable Ryan isn't in the station. I can't say where she is.'

With bitter irony, almost a repeat of the words he had asked the AB to say to her. 'Will you tell her Felix phoned to say he's belatedly understood.'

'All right.' The line went dead.

He hurried back to the gangway, climbed it. 'OK, hoist away.' He made his way for'd to the bows. The phone, rigged for undocking, rang.

'I'm grateful you've finally managed to turn up at your station, chief,' the captain said with juvenile sarcasm.

'Sorry, sir, I had—' The line went dead and he replaced the receiver.

'Single up,' came the order through a loud hailer.

'Single up to one headrope and backspring,' he said.

The carpenter stood by the controls of the windlass as the two seamen uncoiled to one turn the outer headrope and allowed it to slack away until almost trailing in the water. Ashore, a man lifted off the bight from the bollard and let it fall. The rope was wound twice around the windlass drum and the carpenter set this revolving.

'Let go the port headrope.'

This was hauled aboard.

'Hold fast the backspring.'

The ship was moving forward and the backspring tautened until it was under considerable tension.

'Slack a little,' he ordered.

The two hands very carefully – if a wire under strain parted, it could lash back and slice off a leg – let the backspring work around the bollard; it made popping noises as it did so.

There was a shout from the bridge. 'Hold fast the backspring.'

He watched the wire. It was beginning to smoke. 'Slack a little more.'

The phone rang. 'Chief, when I give the order to hold fast, I mean, hold fast.'

'I had to slack or the wire would have parted.'

They slowly swung out from the quayside.

'Let go the backspring.'

The hands eased the wire until it could be released ashore; the windlass hauled it in and it was laid up and down the deck, to be stowed later.

Dunn entered the captain's cabin. 'You wanted me, sir?'

'Please sit.'

He sat.

'I thought it would be a good idea to have a chat and remove the chance of misunderstanding. But first, would you like a drink?'

'No, thank you.'

'Good. I don't approve of drinking at sea.'

They were going to have to be careful with their prelunch pink gins.

'I like to run a tidy ship; in the navy, I believe it is called a tiddly ship. What would you say constitutes a tidy ship?'

'One in which everything proceeds smoothly.'

'So would you call this a tidy ship?'

'I've tried to make her so.'

'But perhaps not tried hard enough. When a ship is on the point of sailing, it does not behove the chief officer to go ashore rather than to his docking station.'

'I'm sorry, sir, but I had an extremely important phone call to make and the shore phone had been removed.'

'If it was that important, shouldn't you have made it earlier?'

'Probably.'

'There is another matter. When I give an order, I expect it to be carried out. A not unreasonable expectation, I hope you'll agree?'

'If you're referring to the backspring—'

'Twice, you were told to hold fast, twice you slacked away. This caused the pilot considerable concern.'

'He'd allowed too much way. If I hadn't slacked, the wire would have parted.'

'He considered it would take the strain.'

'He couldn't judge as clearly as I could on deck.'

'Of course, if you were that certain . . . Decisions taken at such moments are difficult . . . I'm glad we've cleared the air. Bring a problem out into the open and one can solve it, leave it hidden and it festers. You'll agree?'

'Up to a point.'

'You are a cautious man?'

'When there is need to be cautious.'

'And at other times – as you showed when you went ashore to make that phone call – wild and impetuous.' The captain smiled.

The smile of a bankrupt man applying for credit, Dunn thought.

'Have I mentioned that Captain Barton spoke highly of you?'

'You did, yes sir. It's good to hear.'

'So I'm sure we'll work well together and run a tight, happy ship.'

Dunn left, equally certain that soon she would be an unhappy ship.

Twenty-Two

They had loaded coffee, cloves and vanilla in Tomasina and were now heading for Cape Town, a port infrequently used by the company's ships. As he made his way up to the bridge, using the handrail to steady himself because the ship was pitching, Dunn wondered if the captain was still concerning himself with every detail of approach and pilotage because he had not previously commanded a ship docking there. A man who lacked confidence.

He entered the chartroom, read the 12–4 entry in the log book and then the captain's orders – which more resembled requests – briefly studied the chart, crossed to the barometer, swinging in its gimbals, and checked the reading. Still going down. The most recent weather report received in the wireless office forecast moderate to heavy gales.

He went through to the wheelhouse and out on to the starboard wing.

'Morning, chief,' the third said, with the cheerfulness of someone about to go off watch and down to his bunk.

Dunn yawned.

'Sea's getting up. I reckon we're in for a blow.'

'Now give me the bad news.'

'The old man wants calling at six which means you'll have him to talk to.'

Dunn yawned again.

'What do you reckon?'

'Things will always get rougher before they get smoother.'

'I mean, about the old man.'

'I don't reckon anything.' Moran would be disappointed by his reticence in criticizing the captain, but authority had to appear to be respected even when it was not.

'How long d'you reckon we'll be in Cape Town?'

'A week.' The ship pitched heavily and Dunn grabbed hold of the engine-room telegraph for support.

'I've not been there before. Have you?'

'Two, three years back.'

'What's it like?'

'Much like any other major port.'

'You don't make it sound very entertaining.'

'I've long since given up judging a port by the females' eagerness.'

'My uncle always said that old age was the worst disease of all. I'm off, then.'

'Before you've handed over?'

The third chuckled. 'Sir, I humbly beg to report we are steering two three five, revs are seventy-six, compass error of one east could not be checked due to overcast skies, and there's nothing in sight.'

'Thank you, Mr Moran.'

The ship was caught off rhythm by one wave and her bows thrust down into the next one; water rose to be shredded by the wind and the spray swept aft to drum against the wheelhouse bulkhead and ports and caused them to swear because they had not ducked in time.

'I need wet gear,' Dunn said. 'Would you nip down and get it for me?'

'Why not get the stand-by to do that?'

'Do you never feel the urge to help someone?'

'Only rarely and when it happens, I lie down.'

Dunn went into the wheelhouse, followed by Moran, who made his way along the short alleyway and down the companionway. As Dunn picked up one of the sandwiches from the tray on the for'd working surface, the relief helmsman entered the wheelhouse. There was a brief murmur of conversation, then the relieved AB reported their course.

'Do something for me when you get below,' Dunn said. 'Tell the stand-by to bring up my oilskins and sou'wester from my cabin.'

'Aye, aye, sir.'

The sandwich was stale, the tea weak and tepid, but nevertheless he felt a little life creep back into himself.

The gyro was ticking irregularly.

'Are you having trouble holding course?' he asked.

'She's a bit lively, sir.'

'Keep her as tight as you can.'

An unnecessary order since that was the helmsman's job. His mind flicked back to when he had discussed unnecessary orders with Helen . . .

Out on the starboard wing, he rested his forearms on the dodger and stared into the blackness ahead. He had hoped Helen would understand his cryptic message and respond to it. The company office could have given her the dates and addresses for letters; she could have sent a cable . . . Had she ever received his message? Had she decided to make no response because his accusations had caused too much bitter resentment? He could have sent her a cable to seek the answers, but – absurdly – had not because then he could continue to believe that whatever the cause of her silence, it was not the worst possibility.

He heard the hiss of oncoming spray and ducked. As he straightened up, the stand-by came out of the wheelhouse and handed him his foul-weather gear. He thanked the man and pulled on oilskins and sou'wester just in time to fend off more spray. Even in the short time he had been on the bridge, the sea had risen.

He went through to the chart room and read the barometer. Pressure was still dropping. The third had suggested they were in for a blow. In his judgment, they were in for a full-bodied gale.

* * *

The captain stood in front of the clear-view port, the glass of which spun so quickly that the fiercest spray only temporarily obscured vision. 'What force do you give the wind, chief?'

Dunn, who had just come in from the lee wing, said: 'Eight to nine, sir.'

'Call it ten for the log.'

Not an unusual order. Wind strength was increased in the official record in order to justify insurance claims for storm damage.

The captain looked up at the ship's heading repeater on the for'd bulkhead. 'You're nine degrees off course.'

'She's difficult to keep steady, sir,' the helmsman said.

As if to underline his words, a wave caught their bows and forced them several degrees to port. The helmsman added starboard wheel, his lips moving to silent curses as he did so. Another wave, its crest curling, slammed into their bows and sent them further to port.

'Can't you steer?' the captain demanded shrilly.

Dunn said: 'It is a very confused and difficult sea.'

'Not for a competent helmsman.'

He wondered what cat's-cradle of a wake they'd leave if the captain was at the wheel.

The bows rose to a high crest and the captain was caught off balance and ended up against the standard compass.

'Sir,' Dunn said, 'I suggest we slow.'

'You think this is some flat-bottomed coaster?'

'She's beginning to move heavily and Captain Sewell always slowed in such conditions because, as he said, she's old and—'

'It has escaped your attention that I am now in command? Maintain speed.'

Dunn mentally shrugged his shoulders.

Twenty-Three

By eight, the wind was a genuine force 9 and the sea was a confusion of rearing, breaking water which lacked rhythm, so that the *Hakota* constantly thrust her bows into waves and green water swept over them to explode against the windlass and hatch coaming at number one or she rose up to come sweeping down with a twisting motion, shuddering from stem to stern.

The third checked the barometer. 'Why isn't the old man slowing down?'

'Doesn't think it necessary,' Dunn replied briefly.

'Is he a zombie?'

'It's his judgment to make.'

'She's too ancient and worn out to take these seas at our present speed.'

The relieved helmsman appeared in the doorway. 'Steering two thirty-five, sir. Occasionally,' he added sotto voce.

Dunn thanked him. He left.

'Chief, can't you suggest we drop down to half speed,' the third said.

'I did, earlier on.'

'So what did he say?'

'I told you a moment ago.'

'Can't he feel she's working too hard?'

The helmsman failed to counter the seas, the *Hakota*'s bows surged to starboard and the succeeding wave caught them at an angle, so she corkscrewed up and down. Dunn managed to grab the central pillar, but the third skidded into the bulkhead with a force that made him cry out. The fiddle of the chart table had been raised, but chart, pencils, parallel rulers, rubber, and a Notice to Mariners swept into it with sufficient force that everything except the chart fell to the deck. The sound reached them of the drumming of heavy spray against the for'd wheelhouse bulkhead.

'I'll go below and speak to him again,' Dunn said, as he released his hold on the pillar.

'Tell him I've bust my shoulder.'

'I doubt he'll be interested.'

He left the wheelhouse and went down the companionway, having to fend himself first off one bulkhead, then off the other.

The captain, reading a book, was seated on one of the chairs secured to the deck. He looked up. 'I was just about to call you, chief, to ask if you know where one picks up the pilot in Cape Town these days?'

'I don't. I think—'

'I thought you'd sailed there?'

'A time back, sir, and I believe the pilot station has been changed . . . The barometer's still dropping, the sea's growing, and in my judgment we ought to slow.'

'Captain Sewell may have slowed when the first white horse appeared, I do not.'

The captain's stupid stubbornness caused Dunn to forget the need of tact. 'Can't you feel how she's labouring? She's old and her hull plates—'

'My orders are quite clear. Because of Captain Sewell's death, the ship's prolonged stay in Coalpool incurred very considerable extra costs to the company which makes it more important than ever we keep to our schedule. We are due in Cape Town on Saturday and that is when we will arrive.'

'You'll risk the ship and our lives just to please the company?'

'I strongly object to that remark.'

'Object, but if we keep steaming at this speed and the storm strengthens, there could be trouble.'

'I am not in the habit of having my orders and judgment questioned by my junior officers.'

'You can't understand it's the sea that's questioning your judgment?'

'It is quite obvious you have mistaken my attitude to command. I consider friendly relationships with my officers to be desirable, but that does not mean I am prepared to suffer insolence. I regret I shall have to inform Captain Barton that there is reason to doubt his high opinion of you.'

'Captain Barton will understand what it seems you cannot.'

'Enough!'

Dunn turned and left.

By four in the morning, contrary to expectations, both wind and sea had dropped and the *Hakota* was no longer stressed. At six thirty, as daylight was providing a horizon, the captain came out of the wheelhouse on to the port wing.

'I imagine you no longer wish to reduce speed, chief?'

'No, sir.'

'Have you checked for damage?'

'The bosun has.'

'And?'

'There is none.'

'Your judgment seems to have been at fault.'

Dunn stared ahead.

The captain spoke to Dunn on the wing. 'Chief, the boatdeck needs holystoning. I like to have a smart ship.'

'I've told the bosun to finish red-leading and painting the davits before anything else.'

'You did not understand what I've just said?'

Dunn was tempted to explain in simple terms that to make certain the davits were clear of rust and in good working order was of far more importance than holystoning the deck, but accepted his words would merely exacerbate the captain's ill humour.

The captain went into the wheelhouse.

Dunn leaned on the dodger. The captain had the character of a small man promoted beyond his worth and would almost certainly write a damning report on him as a way of getting his own back for the contempt he, Dunn, had too clearly shown for his seamanship and command. How badly would that affect his career? Would Captain Barton's good opinion of him survive?

Asking questions for which there could be no immediate answers was one way of inducing frustration. He began to pace. And suddenly came to an abrupt halt as he tried to make sense of what he saw. A horizon that was no longer sharply defined and regular, but like the uneven crests of a mountain range. Then, with disbelieving certainty, he accepted he was looking at a distant wave; a superwave, something which until very recently had been derided by shore experts as no more than the fertile imagination of seamen who believed in mermaids. 'Starboard ten,' he shouted.

He crossed to the engine-room telegraph and brought both handles up to Dead Slow Ahead. If they met the wave bow on and at very slow speed, they might survive; if not, they would be rolled over. There was no immediate jangling of bells and the confirming indicators remained at Full Ahead. He pushed the handles down to Full Ahead, then back up to Dead Slow Ahead, repeated this a second time. The bells assured him the engine-room staff now understood the order had not been a mistake. As they came round, the wall of water began to turn into a mountain.

The captain hurried out of the wheelhouse. 'What the devil's going on? Have you gone—' He stopped as he saw the wave.

'I'll warn the crew.'

The captain said nothing, did nothing.

Dunn raced through the wheelhouse into the chartroom, on the starboard bulkhead of which was the crew address system. Ancient in design, it sometimes worked and sometimes didn't. He lifted the microphone off its hook, pressed the transmit button. 'All hands. All hands. We are approaching a large sea which will move the ship very heavily. Hold on to something fast and keep holding until we are clear.' He went back to the wheelhouse and used the phone to warn the engine-room staff. He stood in front of the standard compass binnacle and stared ahead. 'Starboard . . . 'Midships.' When they were bow on to the oncoming wave, he returned to the wing. 'I've warned all the crew.'

The captain might not have heard. He was holding on to the dodger, his expression fixed.

'Do you know if Sparks is on watch, sir?'

There was no answer.

He hurried into the chartroom and used parallel rulers and dividers to fix a dead reckoning position, which he wrote down on paper. He returned outside and went aft to the wireless cabin. The wireless operator sat at the working surface on which were keyboard, transmitter and receiver; behind him was the automatic SOS receiver. Morse was being transmitted, but he had established it was of no consequence to them. He looked up as Dunn entered.

'Stand by to send an SOS,' Dunn said.

'What the hell's up?'

'A giant wave's heading our way.'

'It's not April the first, is it?'

'Look dead ahead.'

He stood, stepped out on deck. When he returned, his face was tight from shock.

'If we need to send, here's our position.' Dunn put one piece of paper down by the keyboard.

'It . . . it surely can't be that dangerous?'

'That's what we're about to find out.'

Dunn returned to the bridge as, with the irony in which life delighted, some of the clouds parted and a shaft of sunshine reached the sea ahead of them and made it sparkle. He reported to the captain. 'Sparks has our position to transmit if necessary.'

'What's that?'

He repeated what he'd said.

'We've got to turn about.'

'The wave will be running at several times our speed—'

'Hard a port.'

'That's suicide.'

'Do as I order.'

Dunn returned into the wheelhouse and stood by the binnacle.

The captain appeared in the doorway. 'Didn't you hear me?' he shouted. 'Hard a port.'

The helmsman prepared to turn the wheel.

'Steady as you go unless you want to shake hands with Neptune,' Dunn said.

The captain shouted words they could not understand, disappeared. The helmsman began to mutter – whether a prayer or curses, Dunn could not tell. The sea would respond to neither.

They rode one wave which raised their bows. Then they faced a trough so deep it seemed it must reach almost down to the sea bed. For an endless time, the *Hakota* remained horizontal, supported by receding water, then she swept downwards, shuddering, as if a giant's hand had gripped and shaken her. A wall of water crashed over her bows; it twisted the railings into contorted shapes, shifted the windlass off its bed, lifted off tarpaulins and hatch boards on No 1 and flooded the hold, crushed the winch house, lifted off tarpaulins and hatchboards of No 2, swept over No 3 to thunder against the accommodation bulkheads, reached up to the wheelhouse and shattered the ports, swept both Dunn and the helmsman off their feet despite the strength with which they had been holding on to supports.

The wave was past. Dunn, sodden, regained his feet. The helmsman had been temporarily knocked unconscious, but was clearly recovering. The wheelhouse was in shambles with some equipment ripped off the bulkheads, flag lockers reduced to firewood.

He went out on to the port wing. The captain had been hurled the length of the wing and into the bulkhead. His head was at an abnormal angle and blood was staining the deck. Dunn felt for a pulse, unsurprised when he failed to find one.

The second and third came out on to the wing; the second was supporting his left arm with his right. They stared at the captain.

'She's bow down and for'd holds are flooding,' Dunn said. 'I'm going to turn her stern to. Then if we can raise the bows, we may be able to keep any more water out of the holds and pump them dry. Second, if the phone's still working, tell the engine room to empty all for'd tanks and fill all after ones. Third, tell Chippy to cast off the remaining anchor and chain; the bosun, to make certain the boats are ready.'

Holding her stern to the sea was difficult despite skilful use of rudder and screws. The engine room had emptied the for'd tanks, filled the after ones, and begun to pump out

Nos 1 and 2. After considerable effort, the carpenter had let go anchor and chain. Their bows had risen a little, but the screws were still partially out of the water and thrashing it. Nevertheless, on the bridge they gained a measure of confidence, even of optimism.

The indicators on the engine-room telegraphs swung round to Stop and the bells sounded.

'Find out what's happened,' Dunn ordered.

The third hurried into the wheelhouse, returned a moment later. 'Something's gone in the engines, but they're not certain what.'

Dunn watched the stern, no longer under the influence of the screws, very slowly swing to starboard. Soon, they lay beam on.

'What the hell are the engineers doing?' the third suddenly said violently.

'Their best.' Dunn stared through the wheelhouse port. If the engines weren't soon running, their best would not be good enough.

Calvert came up to the bridge. 'I wondered if you'd like breakfast up here, sir?'

'I would and so would the second and third. Can you manage that?'

'No problem.' He returned below.

Dunn had not thought of food in hours, now he experienced hunger. Eggs and bacon, toast and marmalade, coffee, would make a new man of him. And a new man could enjoy new hope. The engineers would rectify the problem and once more they would be stern to sea and the for'd holds would no longer flood . . .

A dull, thudding sound which rose in pitch as it died away, came from for'd. The hull vibrated. Dunn's optimism and hunger vanished. The watertight bulkhead between two and three had given way under the weight of water. 'Third, ask them below what are the chances of getting the engines working in the next quarter of an hour?'

The third went into the wheelhouse, returned. 'They haven't yet located the trouble so they can't judge.'

He had to assume the engines would not be working again in time to save the *Hakota*. 'Tell Sparks to send the Mayday signal and the bosun to have the crew standing by their boats.'

He stared out to sea. Had it been as rough as on the previous night, the safe launching of the boats would have been very difficult and very dangerous; now, it should merely be difficult and dangerous.

The third returned. 'Sparks is transmitting. He says there are at least two ships close.'

Minutes passed. Minutes during which each man thought, fearfully, angrily, about death.

A phone rang in the wheelhouse. Both the second and third raced to the doorway, collided; the second cried out from the stab of pain in his injured arm. The third continued inboard. His report was brief. 'The engine room have identified the problem, but it'll take at least six hours to repair.'

Dunn stared for'd. The bows had dropped more and now each wave swirled across the deck and Nos 1 and 2; because of the collapsed bulkhead, No 3 was filling fast. They did not have six hours . . .

The ship suddenly vibrated, more heavily than before. A working lifetime at sea decided him she was fast approaching her end. 'Prepare to abandon ship.' The order every captain hoped never to have to give. 'Third, fourth, your boats.' Because the captain was dead, he was now in command of No 4 boat, the only one powered by a diesel engine.

He went to the end of the wing and stared along the hull. Painters had been made fast one thwart aft of each boat's bows, then carried for'd aboard, around stanchions, and back, ensuring that when launched, each boat would sheer outwards and not slam into the ship's hull, and the painter could be released by those in the boat.

'Abandon ship.' His must be the shortest command on record.

Men climbed into the boats and settled on the thwarts. Aboard, others turned the endless screws of the davits to swing the boats out, then stood by the crucifixes, fall ropes in hand, ready to lower.

There was shouting from No 4 boat. Dunn looked aft to see a man attempt to return to the boat-deck, catch his foot on something, try to regain his balance, fail and fall. He screamed as the boat swung to pin him briefly against the hull, then he fell into the sea. His head reappeared when he was abeam of No 6 boat and as he thrashed the water with his arms, he shouted for help before once more going under. There could be no rescue. By the time a boat was in the water, the falls had been released, and the men started to row, he would be swept well astern. In the troubled sea, it would be impossible to sight him from a boat.

The man in command of each boat had to exercise his judgment to make certain the falls were released together on an uprising wave; if only one fall was released before the water receded, the boat would be upended and the crew thrown out.

The six boats were successfully launched. Except for No 4, under power, the crew rowed – clumsily since few had handled an oar before – clear of the hull and gathered on the starboard side. Dunn, on the wing, looked down at the captain's body as it rolled with the ship. Did he throw it over the side, in the travesty of a sea burial? He decided to leave it where it lay. Custom would be observed. The captain would go down with his ship.

He made his way down to the boat deck and aft to the rope ladder which had been used by crew members who had lowered the boats. As he climbed down it, No 4 boat came alongside; two seamen help him board.

The boats kept close together as they watched the *Hakota* sink. A sight to bring a catch to the throat even if she had been a worn-out tramp.

Two hours later, a cruise ship came in sight.

Twenty-Four

Dunn walked into divisional HQ and asked to speak to Tait. Five minutes later, Tait came through a doorway at the far end of the front room and across to where he waited.

'Congratulations on your lucky escape,' Tait said.

'Thanks.' Perhaps they had been lucky, but skill had played its part.

'You've something to tell me?'

'Possibly.' They were like two dogs meeting and each not knowing if the other was intent on trouble.

'We'll use one of the interview rooms.'

He followed Tait along a corridor which smelled of stale humanity and into a square room, painted in two shades of institutional brown, furnished with table, chairs, and a specialized tape recorder. They sat on opposite sides of the table.

'I've come here because of something which happened when we were abandoning ship,' Dunn said.

'I see.'

Tait, he thought, was already deciding this meeting was going to prove of no importance. 'Tucker was in number four boat.'

Tait's manner changed. He leaned forward slightly.

'When the crew boarded the boats, I was on the bridge and so can't vouch for what happened, but members of the boat's crew are agreed that Tucker suddenly struggled to get out of the boat, saying he had to return aboard. The lamptrimmer, who was in command until I boarded, shouted at him not to be a fool, but he said he had to get something he'd forgotten. He went to climb back aboard, tripped, fell, was crushed between boat and hull, landed in the sea. In the circumstances, it was impossible to save him.'

'Did he say what he'd forgotten?'

'No. But he was obviously desperate to retrieve whatever it was. If one's escaping a sinking ship, one doesn't risk going back aboard and being drowned unless something very important is at stake.'

'You're suggesting he was returning for the diamonds?'

'Yes.'

'Surely he would never have forgotten them?'

'One's overriding desire when the order to abandon ship is given is to escape and nothing else matters. It was fright which made him forget them. Then, in the boat, he could believe he was saved and he suddenly remembered them.'

'It's an ingenious theory.'

'But in your opinion, nothing more?'

'The ship was searched and the diamonds were not found.'

'I could hide a thousand diamonds in an old ship like the *Hakota* and you could send a hundred men to search her and they wouldn't find them.'

Tait began to drum on the table with his fingers. 'Was Grose saved?'

'Tucker was the only casualty.'

'Right.'

'What does that mean?'

'It means, Mr Dunn, that I want to think hard about what you've just told me.'

'To decide whether or not to believe me?'

'How to test your theory.'

Dunn stood. 'Is your name Thomas?'

Tait smiled. 'It's Henry Clarence, but in this day and age I normally only admit to Henry.'

* * *

'Sir,' Tait said over the phone, 'I've just had Dunn come into the station.'

'Why?' Campbell asked.

As curt as ever, Tait thought. 'He wanted to tell me about something which happened when the boat sank. Tucker was in a lifeboat that was about to be lowered when he suddenly said he had to get back aboard because he'd forgotten something.'

'What was the something?'

'He didn't say. But as Dunn pointed out, no one's returning aboard a sinking boat unless it's very important.'

'Dunn's suggesting Tucker was returning for the diamonds?'

'Yes.'

'He's hardly likely to have forgotten them.'

'Dunn's reply to that was when one's on a sinking ship, all one thinks about is getting off it. Then, when one's in a lifeboat and there's reason to believe one will be saved, the mind stops panicking and remembers.'

'Dunn's forgotten the ship was searched?'

'He claims he could find a hiding place on a ship which no team would ever find. That could be right. A ship is native land to a seaman, foreign to us.'

'I'm surprised you're prepared to believe him.'

'Why's that?'

'It unfortunately doesn't seem to have occurred to you that he's sharp enough to realize it would be possible to use the sinking of the ship and the death of Tucker to imagine up a claim of innocence.'

'There's one way of testing his claim.'

'Which is?'

'If Grose lied to provide Tucker with an alibi, he'll have been promised a heavy bribe since murder was involved. But Tucker won't have been able to pay the bribe until he sold the diamonds. Grose now knows he can wait until doomsday, but he won't be receiving a farthing. So if he's questioned again, is made very much aware of our suspicions and the danger they place him in, then it's odds on he'll remember he was mistaken about the alibi he provided Tucker.'

'Interview him and let me know the result,' Campbell said before he rang off without bothering to thank him for the information.

Tait began to drum his fingers on the desk. Assuming Tucker's guilt could be presumed from the circumstantial evidence, then his and Campbell's flimsies would not suffer black marks. But how to ensure Campbell did not claim all the credit for solving the case?

The taxi stopped in front of Rosehip Cottage. Dunn, without baggage because everything aboard had been lost, paid the driver, opened the gate, walked along the brick path, unlocked the front door, stepped into the hall. There was a smell of cooking.

Presuming squatters had moved in, he crossed to the kitchen, prepared for argument, perhaps even violence. The oven was switched on and the working surface by the window bore evidence of the preparation of food . . .

'I hope you like steak and kidney pie?' Helen said.

He swung round to face her in the doorway of the dining room. 'What . . . why . . . ?'

'Why? Because the Chinese say man with full belly sees golden world.' She came forward, put her arms around him, kissed him, and murmured how she'd been so bitterly angered by his accusation, she'd ignored his message, but when she'd heard on the news that the *Hakota* had sunk but he had been saved, she'd suddenly understood how ridiculously unimportant her resentment had been.